Something Haunted

Sarah Dale

For, and with, David.

Printed in the United States of America

This edition Printed, 2020

ISBN-13: 978-1-948661-74-4
AISN: 978-1-948661-73-7

© *Sarah Dale*, 2020

Cover Art © *Janina Franck*, 2020
Editing © *M.T. Freelance Designs*, 2020
Interior Design © *Foundation Formatting*, 2020

Note from the author

The names, places and events surrounding Charles Starkweather and Caril Ann Fugate's murder spree in late 1957 and early 1958 are real and historically accurate per the Author's research. Many of the places in Lincoln used in the story are real places, although the author has taken creative license with the details of the settings.

The names of each of their victims and the details of their lives as researched and expressed by Angie are also real and as accurately and lovingly portrayed as the Author was able. It is the hope of the Author that in a small way, not only the horror of that time is reflected here, but also the beauty and importance of the lives lost.

Everything else is fiction.

Much is made of the criminals in our culture. One bad or broken person who acts out with violent passion can be seen as the most important actor in a tragedy. But there is always balance.

For Robert Colvert, Marion Bartlett, Velda Bartlett and little Betty Jean. For August Meyer, Bobby Jensen, Carol King, C. Lauer Ward and Clara Ward, Lillian Fencl and for Merle Collison.

If you're reading this, you've found my hidey hole. I've been keeping journals of our adventures for more than three decades now, and up until last week, I believed them to be safely hidden in my home. Now, everything has changed.

It's not that I fear they will be discovered; rather the opposite. I fear they'll be destroyed, and the record of our life's work would simply disappear.

I'm putting them here for safekeeping. I've spent enough hours in this library to know what gets tended regularly, and what gets regularly overlooked. So if you're finding this now, you must be doing a deep clean, or maybe, just maybe, the City has come together with the funds for a new building, and this one is being cleared out.

Do me a favor. Do what you can to keep these safe. Tuck them back away, or move them if you need to, but don't let them be destroyed.

And if it's you they're meant for, then, good luck, my friend. You're going to need it.

The events of the fall of 1983 were tangled up with both our introduction to the world of junior high and the dark history of Lincoln. Looking back on my journals from that time, I can't tell which I found most difficult — dealing with the natural or the supernatural.

Junior high is hard. Being thirteen is hard. And meeting up with the ghosts of the past and sending them back to whatever hell they came from is really freaking hard.

I think the greatest lesson I learned from all of it, was that even in times of the greatest uncertainty, the times when you doubt yourself and everyone around you the most, it's crucial to trust in your friends. Without Jenny and David, without Mr. Rakow and Jen's mom, Lorraine; without all of us together, we wouldn't have made it through.

Also, no matter how cool you try to keep

things, blowing up a big portion of the school will gain you a reputation of sorts.

My dad hollered at me as I was rocketing out the front door. "Angie! Are you on your way to Jenny's?"

"Yep!" I paused, listening over one shoulder and tugging at the strap of my backpack.

"Ok, keep an eye on the weather. If the sirens go off, head for the basement. If your mother and I have to go out, we'll call you at Jenny's and let you know. Do you have the handheld?"

I craned my neck to see the sky. The distinctively greenish cast to the light was a good indicator. We'd have some severe weather tonight.

"Ok Dad, be careful - and wear your hard hats! Yes, the radio is in my backpack. Love you!"

"Love you too. Stay in touch!"

My parents were storm spotters. It was something they'd gotten into through their Ham Radio Operators club. At first, when they would both go out and stand on hilltops in bad weather looking for tornadic activity while my sister and I cowered in our basement alone, it seemed weird and lonely. Before long though, we realized it was a pretty fair expression of their good faith in us, and we started to feel pretty pleased with ourselves about the whole thing.

By now, it was old hat.

I jogged down the street toward Jen's, thinking far more about the first day of school than about storms.

It was our last weekend of summer, and as usual, Jenny, David and I had made plans. I was almost to Jen's when I spotted David approaching. He had stopped his bike and was grinning at me. Even from this distance, I could see the challenge in his eyes.

He was a full block away from Jenny's driveway, near the bottom of the hill. I had just over half a block of straightaway, but I was on foot.

He held up one fist and pumped, once - I got ready, twice - I clenched my fists and gulped air. On three, he jumped on the pedal, cranking his bike up the hill and I took off at a sprint.

A few months ago, there would have been no point

in this. He'd have won, hands down, every time. This summer was different. After our harrowing adventure on the last day of school, when the three of us had to escape David's mom's newly undead boyfriend and the demon that had possessed him, things had changed a bit.

The three of us had spent weeks recovering from our injuries - my broken arm, Jenny's skewered leg, and worst of all, David's eye. He'd had to wait about three weeks after the surgery before they could fit him with a glass eye, during which time there had been an inordinate number of pirate jokes.

Once we were all on our feet though, Mr. Rakow lost no time in getting us moving. First, it was long walks with him and Shadow at Wilderness Park. Those hikes weren't just about getting our bodies healthy; it was also a conveniently private way to give us a crash course in the supernatural.

Mr. Rakow had begun to learn these disturbing truths when he was in Vietnam. He hoped returning home and leaving the war and unrest behind him would mean the end of the terrifying apparitions, but unfortunately, that was not the case.

He told us stories of demons, monsters and even a sea serpent. For reasons unbeknownst to him, Mr. Rakow said that a few folks could see the reality of these assorted beasties, and the rest simply couldn't. They just looked right in the face of evil and … didn't see.

Sometimes people would pass the horrors off as animals, or psychotic criminals. Sometimes people didn't seem to register them at all.

He told us the story of being on a riverboat, in the Mekong Delta, along with thirty other soldiers, and watching off the side as a two-headed, many-eyed river monster lifted its heads out of the murky water and glared balefully at them as they passed. Mr. Rakow said the thing was easily thirty feet long. He got an excellent view of it as they floated by, scaly humps rising and lowering out of the water until finally, he caught a glimpse of its tail.

Only one other person saw anything, he said. A Navy kid from North Carolina. Mr. Rakow caught sight of him, pale, wide-eyed, staring at the thing. He and the sailor made eye contact briefly and then proceeded to ignore each other studiously for the remainder of the journey.

They never once spoke of it.

The first time Mr. Rakow actually had to do battle with a non-human, he was on a foot patrol with his squad, and they were attacked by a small group of enemy soldiers, wearing an unusual emblem on their uniforms - a stylized golden dragon.

Despite being outnumbered and outgunned by the US Army squad, the skirmish was a bloody one. All but two of his guys were killed.

Mr. Rakow and the other surviving member of his squad, a badass boy from Tennessee, wound up together, facing the final enemy soldier. Mr. Rakow said he was never really sure what his Sergeant saw in the last moments of that battle, but he realized that the dragon emblem wasn't merely a decoration. In the dim, hazy light, he watched the enemy soldier's form change and shift from human to something else.

It never entirely lost its human shape, but its visage changed. A scaly creature with glowing eyes seemed to come and go, obscuring the soldier's human features with teeth and scales. Its strength was immense. It took every dirty trick and backup weapon the two of them could muster to take the creature down, and that was after it had sustained significant damage. In the end, it was Sgt. Brimer, the Tennessee boy, who ended the fight by dint of beheading the thing with his machete.

They sat together afterward. Mr. Rakow said he watched as Sgt. Brimer clean the glistening gold scales off his knife, not seeming to realize what he was doing at all.

In all the years he'd been back in the US, he'd only ever spoken of the things he'd seen to one person.

"Who was that?" I asked him gently. He seemed so sad when he said it.

"Her name was Joan. I met her in San Francisco."

"Where is she now?" Jenny asked carefully.

He didn't answer. We let it drop.

Once Mr. Rakow detected that we still had energy left after one of these long hikes, our training started in earnest. Rather than walking, he had us running - both in the woods and on sidewalks and bike paths. Once we got cocky with that, he started loading us up with backpacks full of heavy things. D-cell batteries wrapped in tea towels was one of his favorites.

He talked about tactics, too. We learned to observe our surroundings with an eye to not only escape routes but also strategizing and identifying items that could be used as weapons if needed.

David was best at improvising weapons. Jenny, who was already fast and strong, became even more impressively so. The strategy was my strong point. It got so every step I took, I was finding myself almost obsessively scanning - looking for high ground, escape routes and possible traps.

There was no doubt that my physical skills improved, but truthfully, I had nowhere to go but up, so that wasn't saying much. But still, three months ago, I wouldn't have stood a chance against David, even with a huge advantage. Today was a new day.

I wished like hell I'd worn tennies instead of flip-flops, but I didn't stop, and I didn't take my eyes off David. I matched his ferocious grin with one of my own.

He was standing up on the pedals, bearing down with all his weight. I heard the bang of a screen door. Jen and Jon tumbled out onto the porch and started cheering us on. I poured on the gas. My backpack flopped and banged against my back. The muscles in my legs burned. My eyes were locked on David's. It was going to be close.

"C'mon Angie! You can do it!" hollered Jenny.

"Go Go Go!" yelled Jon.

I was one driveway away, maybe forty feet to go. David was at the corner. Thirty feet … twenty feet … ten.

We were both going full tilt. A collision seemed unavoidable. Jen and Jon were jumping around screaming their heads off.

And ... yep. You guessed it. It's my thing. My toe caught on a spot where a tree root had pushed up the sidewalk, and I went flying.

Fortunately, Jen and I had been training for just such a disaster.

"ROLL!" she shouted.

I rolled. Lucky for me, I hit the grass. Then, curled up like an ungainly roly-poly bug, I somersaulted to the base of the driveway ... and stopped with my nose half an inch from David's front tire.

It was a tie.

I stood, brushed myself off and high-fived David. Our shouts and laughter brought Jen's mom to the door, tall glass of iced tea in her hand. She frowned when she spotted my scuffed-up hands and knees. "You okay, Angie girl?"

"Yeah, mom!" I flashed her a smile. "Just learning some new superhero tricks!" She grinned.

We'd had several long conversations with Mr. Rakow about who we should tell about this new extra-curricular activity we were taking on. His feeling was that unless our parents were among that small portion of the population who could see the supernatural boogeymen for what they were, it was pointless to try to explain.

That meant Jenny's mom was in. She and Mr. Rakow had known about each other for a long time, it seemed. Jen's mom, Lorraine, wasn't one to go out of her way to fight any of the evils she was able to see. According to him, though, there were plenty of instances where she'd used her knowledge to steer innocent bystanders out of the way, and there was at least one member of the local police force with whom she collaborated behind the scenes.

David had no problem not telling his mom. She was still recovering from the accident on the last day of school, and there was some doubt about whether she would be able to come home at all. Jen's mom had arranged for David to stay with them for the time being, and Mr. Rakow was helping him take care of the house.

My folks were a different story. As of yet, they hadn't shown any indication of being aware. If anyone would be, I'd think my dad, particularly, would be a prime contender. He was a professor of Comparative Religions and Ethics at the Wesleyan University here in town. But, thus far, neither he nor my mom had shown any insight or particular leanings toward the subject. So, for now, at least, those in the know were just Jen's mom and Mr. Rakow.

I think Jon knew. He and Jen had a whole lot of that twin bond thing going on. But he never let on. He was just there when we needed a fourth for some workout or training game Mr. Rakow suggested and gone when we talked about monster stuff.

One of Jon's many friends showed up then, wanting us to shoot hoops at the school while the weather held.

"What about the new idea you wanted to tell us, Ang?" David whispered.

"Don't worry; it'll keep 'til later. Let's go!"

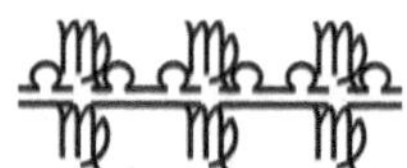

Big fat raindrops had started to fall when we piled back into Jen's kitchen an hour later, ravenous. Her mom had made lasagna and kept it warm in the oven for us.

"Your mom is so bitchin'," I mumbled around a mouthful of cheese and sauce.

Jen put her hand down on the table and looked at me sternly. "No valley-girl speak. We agreed."

I sighed. I'd inadvertently picked it up from my sister's friends. I'd initially thought it harmless, but Jen and

David had forbidden it outright on the grounds that it was abjectly stupid and annoying. I was willing to let them have their victory.

"So, what is the plan for tonight?" Jen asked as we headed downstairs, leaving Jon to decimate the last of the lasagna.

"Information gathering," I responded.

"Did you discover some new ancient tome?" she asked, winking.

My obsession with uncovering information about our experience with Mitch, the mostly dead, demonically-possessed jerkface, had, among other things, expanded my knowledge of other libraries around the world and the joys of interlibrary loans. It also amused my friends, although they were always game to get my summaries once I'd done the heavy lifting.

"Not this time," I said, grabbing my backpack from where I'd tossed it before we left for the playground earlier. "This method is a little bit less orthodox."

"Seance?" Jen guessed.

"Ritual sacrifice?" David supplied.

"Vision quest?" Jen quipped, grinning wickedly at David. Once they got started with the one-upping, they were hard to stop. I rolled my eyes and let them go at it until they were tired, which happened sometime after bloodletting, scarification, and fire walking.

"I can't believe you skipped right over this one. Scarification? Really? Gag me!" The two of them had flopped down on the couch, laughing and snorting.

"So, what is it?" David asked, grinning.

I theatrically pulled the Ouija board out of my backpack like I was one of Bob's beauties on The Price is Right.

"Ooooh, nice - old school! David admired the game. It really was nice. I'd found it at the thrift store, but it was homemade. Someone had carefully etched the letters onto the wooden board. It was elegant, almost artistic. The planchette had been carefully cut out with a jigsaw, and the clear stone that targeted the letters was faceted, like some variety of crystal.

Outside, lightning flashed, and thunder cracked, loudly. The wail of tornado sirens cranked up, and we heard Jen's mom shut off the TV upstairs and make her way down. I set the Ouija board back in its box and left the rest of my stuff on the card table at the far end of the basement, furthest from the TV, while Jen tuned in the local weather.

"Have you heard from my mom and dad?" I asked as Jen's mom came into the room.

"I sure did, Angie girl." That's what she always called me. She was the only one who did, which made it sound uniquely sweet. "They called while I was on the other line. Your mom said they were headed north of town, out Highway 77. She says the system is moving fast, so they shouldn't need to be out for too long."

"Ok, cool. Did they call my sister too? Or am I supposed to do that?"

"She said they did, and that she's spending the night at … Heather's? Does that sound right?"

"Yeah, that was the plan."

The beeping from the TV overrode any further conversation. The weather guy from the local station was on the air.

"Thanks for tuning in, folks. We are currently tracking a storm system north of Lincoln. Spotters have reported rotation five miles south of Seward, moving northeast. The National Weather Service has issued a tornado warning for Seward, northern Lancaster and Saunders counties effective until 9:20 p.m. If you are in any of the affected counties, please take shelter immediately. Move to the lowest level of your home…"

I examined the radar on the screen, wondering exactly where my parents were at the moment; hoping they were safe.

"We're getting reports of golf ball-sized hail in…" he was interrupted by a commotion in the newsroom.

"Ladies and gentlemen, our Tower Cam is showing evidence of wind-driven debris here in town … yes, do they have it?" he asked someone off screen. "Our weekend meteorologist, Megan, has identified a disturbance very close to the station - right across the street, in fact. While we get the video to you at home, Megan, can you describe what you're seeing, please?"

"Ken, I see evidence of rotation, but it's a very … extremely, small disturbance." She sounded like she was having a hard time believing what she was seeing. "It's making its way through Wyuka cemetery right now, on a northeasterly trajectory."

"I'm checking the radar, Megan, I don't see anything corresponding here…"

"Right, Ken. As I said, this is a tiny disturbance. Maybe three to five meters wide, and maybe seven to ten high. More along the lines of a whirlwind, or a gustnado."

A fuzzy picture slowly clarified on the screen.

"Okay, Megan, we've got the Tower Cam shot up!"

I held my breath while the video materialized. A high up shot from the top of the TV station's tower showed the cemetery directly to their south. Whatever the disturbance was, it was obviously fairly small. You could clearly see the boundaries of the little storm moving between trees and white splotches that must have been headstones. And it was most definitely rotating.

"It's doing quite a little dance!" Megan noted, almost to herself. Then she put her broadcaster voice back on, "It's still moving northeasterly through the cemetery at a good clip. If it doesn't dissipate, it should be outside the fence in a moment and headed our way, Ken!"

Over her microphone, the scuffle and bluster in the newsroom were partly audible. We distinctly heard someone saying, *If you don't absolutely need to be here right now, get downstairs!*

"Please take shelter at once," Megan continued in a calm but fascinated tone. "Central and northeastern Lincoln, we have visual of a…" she paused, "a cloud with rotation within city limits. Anyone in the vicinity of 48th and Vine streets should take cover immediately in the lowest level of your home or business."

In Jen's basement, we were all glued to the TV.

"What is it?" David asked. "It's not a real tornado, right? It's way too small!"

Jen glanced over at me. "Weren't you telling me one time about weird tornadoes?"

I mentally flipped through the conversations I'd had on the topic with my dad until something clicked. "Yeah! Dad was telling me about some PBS special. It had something to do with those, what did she just call them, gustnadoes? But I'm not sure this is the same thing…" I trailed off and looked over my shoulder. Something was rattling around behind us, and then we all heard a heavy thud. Jen and David raced toward the sound with Jen's mom and me close behind.

"Is that window open?" Lorraine asked.

"No, that's not it!" David and Jenny had stopped stock still in front of the card table where I'd dumped my stuff earlier.

I identified the source of the thud pretty quickly. My unzipped backpack had fallen to the floor, and my stuff was all over. The rattling was coming from the table, and Jen and David were standing, unmoving, in my way. I shoved in between them and froze too.

The Ouija board was *moving*.

Not just a little bit, either. The thing was dancing around, shaking itself free of the box it was still partially inside. The planchette had already juked its way out onto the table, and it was zooming around.

"What the…" I began. Jen's mom put a hand on my shoulder.

"Shhh, Angie girl. Let's watch and see."

Jen's long fingers reached out. I could see what she was aiming for; the board was caught up and trying to free itself from the last corner of the box. Her mom reached out and calmly but firmly grasped Jenny's hand in her own. "Don't touch, love. Watch."

"What's it doing?" David whispered. We all jumped a little as the board gave one final flop and freed itself from the cardboard box. The planchette did a happy little spin and jumped onto the board. We waited, breathlessly.

"Are we supposed to…" I began. Jen's mom's fingers tightened on my shoulder, and the planchette took off.

I pulled the notebook and pen out of my pocket where I always kept it. Yes. I know. I was a giant nerd back then. Still am. You're just going to have to deal.

"Watch close," Jen's mom whispered, leaning over my shoulder. She needn't have worried; everyone's eyes were glued on the spectacle of the planchette break dancing all over the board. Then suddenly it got serious. It paused, then zoomed to the W. I scribbled it down. H … E … R … E

"Where? Where what?" David asked, staring at the planchette.

It had paused, still vibrating madly, but at the sound of his voice, it continued. W … H … O … I … S… T … H … E … R

We stared at one another. Jen's eyes were as wide as saucers. David looked puzzled, but I noticed his body language, too. He seemed poised for a fight. I'm sure I was white as a sheet.

Jen's mom remained calm. As I took a breath to speak, her hand clenched my shoulder tightly.

"Do NOT use anyone's name!" she hissed at us.

I nodded sharply. I knew what she meant. I'd been doing a lot of reading over the summer, everything I could get my hands on about ghosts and demons, magic and the supernatural. A lot of it was crap, but some things were consistent at least, and names were one.

Names had power. It was vital that you guard your name around supernatural creatures. If they had your name, it gave them the advantage and put you at risk. I chose my next words with great care.

"We hear you. We are listening."

The planchette moved again. I … M … B … A … C … K …

We stole wide-eyed glances at each other.

R … Y … O … U … S … T … I … L … L … T … H … E … R … E

"Yes, yes, we're here," I sputtered. The planchette zipped to "GOOD" at the bottom

W … I … L … L … R … E … P … R … T… The planchette stilled.

"Are you still there?" I asked, trying to keep my voice from shaking and secretly hoping the answer was NO.

Nothing.

On the news broadcast behind us, the meteorologists were still buzzing about the gustnado, or whirlwind, whatever it was. Suddenly their words cut through my daze.

"We have a spotter following the disturbance in his vehicle!" I spun around at that, desperately hoping my folks were still north of town. I didn't know what this all meant, but it suddenly seemed very important that they were safe. Then I remembered I had the handheld radio and dove under the card table to grab it out of my backpack.

The TV station was still showing footage from their tower camera. The little whirlwind remained visible, moving away from the station. In the background, we could still hear muffled voices coming from people who weren't on camera, but who were obviously working hard to give Ken and Megan the info they needed to report.

I got the handheld turned on. I wasn't a licensed Ham Radio Operator, so I couldn't transmit, but dad had pre-programmed it to the frequency they used for their Skywarn Net so I could listen in. I heard the voice of the woman calling the net from the TV station. It was my folks' friend Sue, KZ0WBL, in charge of organizing the spotters net from the station today. She would report what her spotters saw to the news crew, and they put it on air.

The next voices we heard were the spotters who were apparently on the ground following the thing. If I wasn't sorely mistaken, one of them was Sue's son Clark! He was only a couple of years older than us, and if I knew anything about anything, his crazy older brother Grant was the one driving them pell-mell through town. Oh man, their mom was going to skin them alive when this was all over.

I turned the volume up on the handheld, ... "This is KZ0BKT. We still have rotation. We're on 48th north-bound, almost to Holdrege. It's headed right for Tastees!"

Tastee Inn & Out was a neighborhood institution, serving questionable loose meat sandwiches and onion chips with a dipping sauce that hooked even sane people at first taste and keep them coming back for more, de-spite their best intentions or their doctors' orders. It was a holdover from the late 1940's, and I don't think they'd updated their signage since then. I crossed my fingers. *Please spare the Tastee Inn,* I whispered silently.

I forced myself to shut up and listen.

"KZ0BLE at Net Control, Keep at a safe distance, KZ0BKT. Are you watching for debris?" came Sue's voice, delicately balanced between professionalism, grudging pride and mom fear.

"KZ0BKO, being *very aware of debris,*" came a some-what lower, slightly defiant voice over the radio. Yep, that was Grant.

"Roger KZ0BKO," retorted their mom.

"This is KZ0BKT," Clark interjected, "The restau-rant sign is knocked down, but the building is still intact. It's in the neighborhood, heading eastbound now."

"Roger KZ0BKT, can you give us a speed estimate?"

"We're going about 25 mph and keeping up with it. It's staying at about 15-20 feet off the ground - I haven't seen a touchdown since it left the cemetery, but it's blast-ing trees right and left. There are a few large limbs down, and there's plenty of smaller debris blowing around. Oops! Somebody just lost an upstairs window!"

Ken's voice continued calmly from the TV, reiterating the location and urging folks in the immediate vicinity to take cover.

"KZ0BKT, give us your location now."

Clark's voice again, "KZ0BKT, location is UNI Park - it has gone around the swimming pool. It's touched down again!" His voice rose with excitement. "It's touched down on the east side of the pool. There goes a picnic table!"

I stared at Jen and David. They returned my gaze. The picnic table on the east side of the pool was the same one Jen had jumped from to get us all inside this summer. It was where we trapped the Mitch thing to the fence, and where he'd finally succumbed.

"KZ0BLE, this is KZ0BKO. It's stopped right on that spot!"

"Roger KZ0BKO, is it dissipating?" his mom asked.

"No, it seems to be increasing, but it's just sitting in that one spot - wait! Now it's moving again - heading out of the park. We're eastbound. It's speeding up, gained some height - just hitting the tops of trees; we're seeing less debris.

David was staring at the TV screen, still showing the shot from the Tower Cam where the disturbance was moving out of range. "It's heading straight for us!"

"Don't worry, kids. We're in the basement. We're safe." Jen's mom's voice was calm, but her brow furrowed.

"KZ0BLE, it's up, way up, 20 to 30 feet above ground," Clark's voice had relaxed a bit, but he was still excited. It's moving north again, up over the college."

"This is KZ0BLE at Net Control, do you mean Wesleyan?" his mom asked for clarification.

"This is KZ0BKT, yes, now it's on," he paused, "Huntington Street. It's moving straight east."

We all breathed a collective sigh of relief. It was

going to miss us.

"Maybe it'll hit the school! David joked.

"This is KZ0BKT; it's dropping again, yep, more debris. There goes somebody's satellite dish! ...and we're crossing 66th Street."

"I hope you had your fingers crossed when you said that," I said to David. "It's headed right for the school!"

"Holy wish fulfillment, Batman!" muttered Jenny.

Clark's voice on the radio again, "This is KZ0BKT, It's on the school grounds now. It has gained height again - no, wait! It's dropping. It's almost past the school, but…"

Suddenly the video feed on the TV shifted from the station's Tower Cam to a live shot.

"Ladies and gentlemen," Ken's voice cut in. He sounded a little annoyed. "We have a reporter on the scene at Robin Mickle Junior High school in northeast Lincoln. What are you seeing, Marlenia?"

"The funnel is still intact, Ken, but it's losing speed. You can see here," she paused, "wait, we have a tail dropping down out of the cloud now." Her shoulder-mounted camera rather unsteadily zoomed in, zeroing in on a small but distinct tail dropping down out of the dark disturbance.

"Do we have another touchdown?" Ken asked.

"I don't think so. I don't believe it's going to reach the ground. It seems to be breaking apart. There is a good deal of debris falling from the cloud…" A flash of something big and black appeared, almost obscured by the dust and wind, but not entirely.

"Wow! Did you see that, Ken?

"Yes! Can you identify it … without getting any closer, Marlenia?" The stern tone in his voice made me wonder if Marlenia had gotten permission to leave the station and take her camera out.

"I'm safe here, Ken," the young reporter said reassuringly. "I can't tell what it is for sure, but it was large. Maybe as big as a car? The funnel is definitely breaking up now, Ken."

"Our spotter is confirming it, Marlenia."

"Yes, there, you can see clearly," she replied, "the funnel has disappeared, and the disturbance is falling apart."

Just then, the planchette rattled again. We rushed over to the table and stared as it spelled out, T ... H ... A ... N ... K ... S ... F ... O ... R ... R ... I ... D ... E. The four of us in Jenny's basement gaped at each other.

"What the hell just happened?" David asked into the sudden silence.

"Thanks for ride?" Jenny asked, peering over my shoulder at my notebook where I'd furiously scribbled the last message. "What does that mean?

"What was that black thing that fell? Could you tell? I asked.

"I think we need to call Mr. Rakow right now." Jen's mom said, heading for the phone.

"Hey, guys! What's up?" Jon emerged from his room with his headphones around his neck, loud music emerging from his Walkman, and rubbing his eyes. He looked around at us curiously. "What'd I miss?"

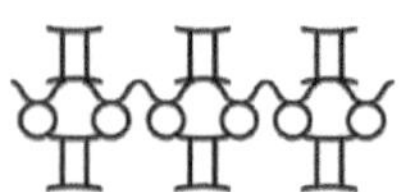

There was no answer at Mr. Rakow's house, so we left a message. We didn't want to try the Ouija board again, without his input, so instead, we stayed up half the night talking. We got maybe an hour's sleep before we had to get up and do Jen's paper route, which was blessedly uneventful that morning.

It was noon before Jen's mom made us get up. We still hadn't heard back from Mr. Rakow, so talk had turned to school, and the topic was hot. There was so much that was going to be different this year - a bigger building to navigate, way more kids, and the biggest concern, trying to get from class to class without getting lost or beat up in the halls between periods.

Jon was chock full of horror stories about gangs of thugs roaming the halls, jocks who would give you swirlies in the boys' locker room, and we'd all heard stories about Mrs. Dietrich, the Dean of Discipline. Of course, Jon had no more first-hand experience than the rest of us, so there was also a whole lot of Jen telling him to shut up.

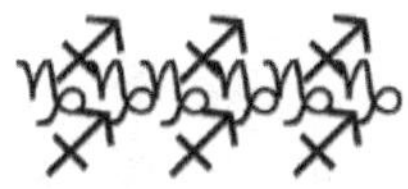

The first morning of 7th grade finally arrived. I was splitting time between being excited and terrified. The harder work and classes didn't scare me so much, I was pretty confident in my academic geekdom, but the potential for doing something stupidly embarrassing was always with me. More space and more people just meant that the inevitable humiliation would have a bigger audience. It was a thrilling thought.

I squashed it down and finished getting ready, so I wouldn't be late. Jen and David were at the corner by my house at exactly 7:35. Jon and his friends were already a block ahead.

We arrived at the school shortly before the first bell. We waded in with the rest of the pool of pre-teen humanity and found our lockers. I lucked out with my combination; it opened the first time. David had to run through his numbers twice, and Jen stared intensely at hers until it surrendered and opened with a meek click.

We didn't have any classes all together. Jen and David had Math and English together; I had Social Studies with Jen and Spanish with David in the afternoons, and we were waiting to find out if we'd lucked out and gotten the same lunch period.

I grinned toothily at them as we separated. Jenny must have felt my tension because she grabbed both my shoulders and pinned me with a stare.

"Don't worry about anything, Ang. You are the smartest girl in the school, and if anybody gives you even a teaspoon of crap, they'll have to deal with all of us."

I smiled an easier smile, relief unwinding some of the tendrils of stress that had hold of me. I made a fist, and the three of us bumped knuckles.

"We still need to figure out some kind of Superhero name," I said in a low voice.

"Yeah, too bad Superfriends is taken," Jen chuckled.

"Besides being totally stupid," David interjected.

"Ok, ok, we'll work on it! How many minutes do we have before the bell?" I asked, craning to see the clock on the wall.

"Three," said David, decisively. I didn't bother to check to see if he was right. His internal clock was always spot on.

"Crap! Gotta run! I have to get down to the orchestra room. See you guys!"

There is a hierarchy of nerdiness in public school music. There are usually a few dudes in the jazz band who might technically qualify as cool, but any potential hipness quotient gets inevitably overshadowed by their bandmates who are, by universal decree, dampeningly nerdy. Next least nerdy are the sorts of singing groups you had to try out for, like swing choir. These groups are mostly upperclassmen; they get to do fun rock-and-roll-ish songs, and they get special clothes for performances, and to skip classes to sing at nursing homes and the mall.

Rocketing downward from there, you see the kids who get to play for school musicals, followed by band, regular choir, and at the deep rocky bottom of the heap, you have the for-the-love-of-god-have-you-no-shame-are-your-parents-making-you-because-you-can't-possibly-like-this-crap nerddom, was orchestra.

It's about this point in our childhoods that we are

first faced with the dilemma - do we shun our nerdiness? Or do we own it? Man. Talk about a musical act fueled by conflict and angst. The Sex Pistols have nothing on your average junior high orchestra kids!

It was the first day, so we got our schedules and music and the procedure for competing for chair placement. I was relieved to discover I was to be the only oboe player. It was a new instrument for me, and I had been nervous about competing against someone who'd been playing one since fourth grade.

While everyone else was milling around, signing up for their chair tryouts, I took a moment to poke around in the equipment storage area. Since I was borrowing an instrument from the school, the rules about taking it home to practice on were a little sticky, and I wanted to see if there was a private corner anyplace where I could sneak in extra practice.

It was a big old room with wooden floors. There were lockers along one wall and larger storage compartments overflowing with music stands, chairs, cases, and boxes. There was even a loft with more storage. It was a creepy cool space, but I was betting the acoustics were awesome.

"Yessssss!" I spotted a likely looking alcove, far enough to the back to be away from any traffic coming in and out, but near enough to the front to be well lit. I wove around stacks of stuff until I reached it. It was perfect. I could just shove that box over a little and...

Goosebumps. I stared at the upraised hairs on my arm that had been toasty warm a moment before. Abruptly, the whole room had gone cold. The kind of cold that makes your bones feel like broken glass and your heart afraid to beat.

I scanned the room as thoroughly as possible without moving an inch. *Freakiest game of freeze tag ever* floated through my thoughts. I instructed my brain to get serious, fast. 'Assess the threat.' It was one of Mr. Rakow's frequent admonitions. Ok. So, what am I dealing with here?

Is this a cold of the old drafty building variety? Or the freaky supernatural kind?

A grunt and a crash from the back of the room disabused me of the notion of a coolant system snafu. 'What are your assets?' Another of Mr. Rakow's lessons. I ticked them off, oboe case, book bag mostly full of school supplies, room full of musical junk. I took a silent step to my left, putting a tall stack of chairs between me and the noise.

"Who's there?" I asked in a low voice.

A wheezy, guttural roar came from the loft. Boxes flew. Somewhere a cymbal crashed. I crouched behind my makeshift bunker and clutched my oboe case to my chest. And then it spoke. The voice was rusty and sharp like the sound was powered by wind blowing through holes rusted in sheet metal. The anger in it was palpable.

Where ... is ... she?!

Gulp.

More boxes exploded down from the loft. Sheet music flew everywhere. Soon kids were going to come in here to find out what was happening, and someone might get hurt. Of course, my current line of thinking was probably going to get *me* hurt. Mr. Rakow's final bit of advice ran through my mind. 'Don't do anything stupid."

"Well, crap. Here goes." I stepped out from behind the little cover I had and stood, in full view of the loft. My legs were quaking, and I was pretty sure I was about to pee my pants. I clenched my fists, took a deep breath and spoke in as steady a voice as I could muster. "Who are you! Who are you looking for?"

A terrifying hiss came from the loft. My feet were rattling on the floor, but I held my ground.

Damn school ... hate school! More things crashed around up in the loft. I started carefully backing away from the sound, trying to get near enough to the door that I could make a run for it if my plan didn't work, but stupid curiosity made me call out one more question.

"What do you want?" My question seemed to

infuriate the thing. A whirlwind of boxes and three or four heavy folding chairs exploded to the floor, one just inches from me. I stumbled backward and barely managed to keep my feet. Cold air rushed all around the room. Amid the crashes in the loft, I heard the thunking, rolling sound of something wooden spilling over the floor. There was a pause, and then a cold, angry laugh filled my ears as something zoomed past my head and smacked into the wall behind me. I turned to see a drumstick, buried four or five inches into the wall.

Crap!

I dropped to the floor and covered my head. A swarm of drumsticks came arrowing down at me from the loft. The voice rasped out, *I ... want ... CAROL!* And with that, everything in the room was in motion - swirling, banging, crashing, and with it, a palpable sense of rage. *CAROL!*

With crap raining down all around me, I started army-crawling toward the door on my knees and elbows, digging into my backpack at the same time. Curse words I didn't even know I knew were emerging from between my clenched teeth.

I grunted in triumph when my hand closed on the item I needed. I rolled to one side, narrowly avoiding a podium that had come sailing down. Once it landed, and my brain restarted out of panic mode, I tucked up behind it, using it as cover, and pulled out my secret weapon.

It was a little gadget we'd cooked up over the summer. It was something like a grenade, in that you yanked the fuse and tossed it. It wasn't an explosive, though. It was a smoke bomb. And it was loaded with not just any smoke. This little doodad burned blessed sage.

Jenny's mom had magicked up the sage for us, chanting prayers over it, although I had yet to suss out what language she was praying in, or to what gods. I was just learning not to be surprised each time Jen's mom produced some fabulous new magical tool. Some grownups, it seemed, had more going on than we initially suspected.

Go figure.

At any rate, she claimed that it should increase the potency of our smoke bomb, which was built to cleanse a space. She said it should work in lots of situations since it wasn't specifically aimed at any one particular varmint, but instead on cleansing the immediate area of any type of bad mojo.

Mr. Rakow and David had worked on the construction. They'd finally settled on using the plastic lemon-shaped bottles lemon juice comes in from the grocery store. They worked best without altering the chemical makeup of the blessed sage, and they had the added benefit of not leaving any actual weapons-grade detritus behind.

David was all for calling them *Easy Peasy Lemon Squeezies*. Jen and I were holding out for a cooler name, like *Mondo Spirit Bomb* or something. Right now, I was less concerned with its name and more concerned that it would work.

I yanked the fuse and tossed it, as best I could up at the loft. I got lucky. Not only did the lemon squeezie make it up into the loft, but it smoked like a carload of stoners at lunch. I was duly impressed.

I heard a gasp from up above, a scuffle, and the sound of things dropping. Then, as the sagey smoke filled the room, a shrill, angry whine began. A rowdy, boisterous stomping sound filled my ears, but this time, it was coming from outside the door, from the rehearsal room.

I'd triggered the fire alarm.

Oops.

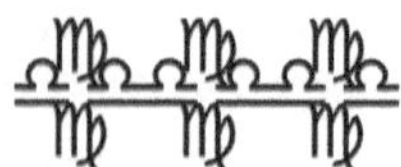

Practically hopping up and down with the adrenaline jazzing madly through my system, I looked around for

Jen or David as I lined up with the rest of my class on the sidewalk outside. No dice, I'd have to fill them in later. I did spot something unusual, though. Just as they rang the all-clear bell and we began filing back inside, I noticed a car cruising slowly past the school. It was an old car, I didn't know exactly what kind, but one you see in old movies with greasers and bobby socksers. It was black underneath a coating of dried mud, and the front piece above the bumper was missing.

It rumbled down the street slowly until it got to the corner past the school, and then with a roar of its big, gas-guzzling engine, it sped off.

I couldn't see a driver.

I bottled up my excitement, worry, and fear for the rest of the day, and by the time the bell rang at 3:00 I was about ready to explode. I dashed out the front door and scanned the melee for Jenny and David.

I caught a glimpse of David, but he was talking to a couple of really big kids, one of whom I knew for sure was on the football team. I'd heard my sister gush about *totally boss #13* all last year, and he and his buddy were both wearing jerseys with their names and numbers emblazoned across the back.

I sighed and scanned the area for Jenny. I finally spotted her, in the center of a group of kids who were all vying for her attention. This was not surprising. Jenny had amazing charisma. Anyone who listened to her talk for more than about thirty seconds ended up with the same look on their face that nearly every one of these kids had at the moment, that dopey, already-half-in-love expression.

I was about to roll my eyes when I noticed that she was actually paying some attention to one of the guys. I couldn't blame her; he was super cute. Dark hair, dark eyes, a rather enigmatic look, definitely not the usual Northeast Lincoln vibe.

I had just begun to feel sorry for myself, standing there like a dork while my friends blew me off, when Jen cut her eyes away from Menudo-boy, saw me, and winked. She extricated herself deftly from her entourage and headed my way.

"Where's David?" she asked.

"Being recruited by the quarterback," I responded dryly. "Something happened in the music room, right before I set off the fire alarm. We need to talk," I said in a low voice.

Her eyes widened. "You set off the…? C'mon." She cocked her head and took off. I followed. Jen strode up to the group of big boys in their blue and silver jerseys who had surrounded David. She pushed her way through a gap in the broad shoulders and snagged David by the collar of his denim jacket. She whispered something in his ear then turned to face the team.

"'Scuse me, fellas," she said, cool as a cucumber. "We need this one's brain right now. You can have his muscles back later." Jenny didn't speak like a lowly seventh grader, meekly addressing the resident football star of the whole school. Jen spoke like she was The Boss in charge of the whole school, speaking professionally with her crew, telling everyone where to stand and what to do, and they totally accepted it. She was amazing.

From my trying-not-to-cower-with-nervousness spot, peeking around an arm as big as my thigh, I saw the expressions of surprised respect on more than one face. David took one look at the pair of us and hitched his backpack up onto his shoulder.

"Gotta jam. See you guys tomorrow."

"I'll tell Coach you'll be there after fourth period tomorrow, Dave," said #13.

"Cool. Thanks, Jason. Later, guys." David nodded at a few of the guys while Jenny did some complicated handshake with #13.

"How do you know that guy, Jen?" I asked once we were out of earshot.

"Long boring story," she replied. "I'll tell you sometime. Now, what's up with you setting off the fire alarm?"

"You did what, Ang?" A look of surprised pride crossed David's face. "What's the scoop?"

I waited until we'd crossed the street and got some space on the other clusters of kids walking home.

"So, apparently, the instrumental music room is haunted, or possessed, or plagued or whatever." I gave them the rundown, and without even making a plan out loud, I saw that we had detoured and were on our way to Mr. Rakow's house.

He was waiting for us on the front porch, with Shadow panting happily by his side. David spared a glance at his house, next door. His mom had transitioned from the regular hospital to a long-term care facility, but we still didn't know if she'd ever been able to come live at home again. Nobody knew as much about traumatic brain injuries back then, as we do now. All we knew then was she was having trouble walking and talking, and it wasn't really getting any better. Everything was in a holding pattern.

Mr. Rakow ushered us into his kitchen and poured iced tea while we launched into the story. He listened carefully, all the way through before he began with questions.

"Tell me again, what you felt right at the beginning?"

"Cold. Super ice cold," I replied, shivering anew at the memory.

"Like, a cold wind?"

"Sort of, but more like, how the cold wind makes you feel in your insides. Like it hurts, from the inside out."

He nodded, stroking his chin. "Then what did you feel?"

"Well, I was pretty freaked out!"

"Yeah, I bet so. What else?" he prodded.

I got what Mr. Rakow was after. He wanted me to separate action from reaction - what was coming AT me rather than FROM me.

"Anger," I replied decisively. Anger, but not mine.

Like, remember that time we were at the burger place with your mom, Jen? And the family with the dad who was such a jerk, and he and the cook started yelling at each other?"

"Yeah, that guy was a total jackass," Jen said, looking at me curiously.

"Remember how after he and the cook started yelling, and then the kids started in too? And then that old guy sitting behind us started in yammering, and then that huge dude came out of the back and made them all leave? It was like it was contagious or something. Once the dad got angry, it like, spread out all over."

"Yeah!" Jen said. "I remember how you pointed over at the waitress, and she was eyeing the wife and taking off her earrings like she was getting ready to wade in and start knocking heads."

"Yeah! It felt like that. Like contagious anger." Mr. Rakow continued to look thoughtful. "Whoever that Carol girl is that ghost is looking for, I sure wouldn't want to be her," I mused.

"What happened next?" Mr. Rakow continued, frowning.

"Well, then I used the lemon squeezie, and the fire alarm went off, and I got the heck out of there! Then we all jammed outside," I bubbled. I was pretty geeked by how well our sage bomb had worked. So much so in fact, that I had forgotten entirely about the car, until just now.

"I don't know if this is connected, Mr. Rakow, but when I was outside for the fire drill, I saw a weird old car."

"Oh yeah? What was weird about it?" he asked.

"Well, it was really old and beat up…"

"Old, like how old?"

"I don't know, my mom always knows what year those old cars are, by their lights or their fins or whatever, but I can never remember.

David chimed in, "Was it like, Starsky and Hutch?"

I grinned. David understood my frames of reference

better than anybody. "No, older. More like the one from Grease, but before they fix it all up, and it was black, not white."

"What was the white car in Grease?" Jenny asked David.

"Ugh, I've only seen that movie once. I'm trying to remember…" David, for all his love of movies, wasn't a fan of musicals.

"It was a Ford," Mr. Rakow said flatly. "A 1948 Ford." We all stared at him. "What? Olivia Newton-John is a fox!"

David grinned wolfishly. Jen and I looked at each other wide-eyed and tried not to laugh. Mr. Rakow cleared his throat and looked at me.

"So, the car was similar to that one?"

"Yeah," I said, trying to swallow my giggles. "I think so."

"Hold on," he got up from the table and went over to the old dining room buffet that served as his desk and file cabinet. From a lower drawer, he withdrew a stack of old calendars and began flipping through them.

David scrambled over to look over his shoulder. "Whoaaa…," he whispered reverently.

Mr. Rakow winked at him. "You can look through those all you want, bud. But later. Let's see if we can iden-tify Miss Angie's mystery car first. He brought a handful of calendars to the table. They ranged from 1938 to 1952 and each month's picture was a different, brand new Ford car or truck.

I flipped past old trucks with rounded hoods, a few convertibles, white-walled tires, and little rearview mir-rors. I scowled, trying to remember details. I remembered thinking the front end looked like some horrid saber-toothed grouper. "The front part was missing…" I mused as I flipped through pages.

"Which front part?" asked Mr. Rakow, peering over my shoulder.

I pointed.

"That's the grille, Ang," said David in his best bored-teacher voice.

"Yeah, yeah," I sing-songed, not rising to his bait. "That's it. It was missing, I think. It just looked dark right there."

"Mr. Rakow's lips tightened. He grabbed one of the calendars from the pile and flipped pages until he found the one he was looking for. He pushed it toward me and asked, "Is this the one?"

"I think so, yes…" I stared at the mossy green-color of the car in the picture, "but black, and very dirty."

"Dirty?" he asked.

"Yeah, like it had been driving in mud," I replied.

"Oh, hell." Mr. Rakow's face was a cloud of dread.

"What?" I asked, nervously.

"I think I may know who our angry ghost is. Saddle up, kids, we're going on a field trip."

"How long?" Jen asked. "Do I need to tell mom we'll be late?"

"This won't take long," Mr. Rakow looked at his watch. "I'll have you all home in plenty of time for your supper."

We piled into Mr. Rakow's old beat up Nova and took off. The ride was short and very quiet. Mr. Rakow wasn't elaborating on his thoughts, and after a few attempts to draw him out, we fell silent. We'd gotten to know him pretty well over the summer, well enough to know that sometimes you could bug him for information, and other times it was best to let him brood first and talk later. This seemed distinctly like one of the latter.

We didn't have to wait long. Within just a few minutes we were pulling into the front entrance of the cemetery. The rear entrance, nearest the television station, was a half mile almost directly north of us. Wyuka was smack dab in the center of town.

The main drag, "O" Street, aka Highway 34, bisected Lincoln into the North and South sides. Almost an entire mile of "O" Street, from 35th St. to 44th St. on the north side, was the cemetery, enclosed by black, wrought iron fencing. Part of that same length, on the south side of "O," was the Catholic cemetery. When we were younger, we used to say you had to hold your breath as you drove past, or your soul would escape your body. I held mine until we reached the driveway, then crossed my fingers for luck as we entered the gates. You know, just in case.

Mr. Rakow drove slowly around inside the cemetery grounds until he spotted what he was looking for. Storm damage.

"You think the school ghost had something to do with that little tornado, don't you?"

He pulled over to the side of one of the winding roads that crisscrossed the cemetery, put the car in park, and turned to meet my gaze.

"Clever girl, Miss Angie. Yes, I do. I've been doing some research on weather patterns and the supernatural."

"There's a connection?" David asked.

"I had a feeling!" Jen exclaimed.

"Where did you do your research?" I demanded.

"Hold your dang horses, the three of you!" He sounded harsh, but I saw the twinkle in his eye. Jabbing a finger at us each in turn, he answered our questions.

"Yes!" and, "I'm not surprised!" and, "I have an interesting library to show you, later." He directed this last at me, and I held back an excited squeak, because, as we have established, I was a big nerd. Still am.

Jenny had already opened her door and was making a beeline across the road toward the torn-up grass and hazard tape. It was clear the groundskeepers had been hard at work. Broken branches had been piled up near the road for pickup, and all the damaged areas had been cordoned off. Repairs were in progress. Several headstones were overturned, and one was cracked, but the most evident damage was the path of torn up grass.

It looked like an out-of-control rototiller had rampaged through the quiet green campus. The path was generally southwest to northeast, as most tornadoes go, but rather than the more or less straight line one usually sees in the wake of a storm, this thing appeared to have disco danced its way through the space. There were loops and swirls, zigzags and backtracks. The grass was a mess. Somebody's sod company was going to make a mint fixing this place up.

I clambered out of the back seat of Mr. Rakow's two-door Chevy, the kind where the front seat folds forward, and if you are an acrobat or a fairy princess, you can exit gracefully. Being neither, I was pleased to avoid a faceplant in the road before getting my feet back under me.

Mr. Rakow was watching Jenny intently as she wended her way along the path the little tornado had taken. I noticed his interest and asked him, "Why are you watching Jen like that?"

"I have a feeling about all of this," he responded quietly, "and I'm curious to see if I'm right."

We had crossed the road and stepped out onto grass dotted with gravestones. David had gotten ahead of Jen, further along the path of devastation. Jen was meandering behind him, pausing to look at a name here, a headstone there. I held back with Mr. Rakow, watching and wondering what he was hoping to see.

Jen stopped abruptly, staring down at one of the small, flat headstones. From behind, I watched her body language change. She drew in on herself, and then blew out a breath and squared her shoulders as if she was forcing herself to look at something unpleasant. I looked at Mr. Rakow. His expression was satisfied, and a little sad.

I ran to Jen's side and arrived just as David did. "Whose grave is it?" he asked. I looked down at the inscription on the stone.

Charles Starkweather
Nov. 25, 1938 - June 25, 1959
Rest in Peace

We all stared at it, eyes wide. The storm had come right past this place, no … not past it, but *around* it, like a dog sniffing at a scent. The storm had paused in its destructive path and danced in a circle around this particular grave.

"Oh, crap," I breathed.

Charles Starkweather was Lincoln's own personal nightmare. When he was nineteen years old, Starkweather had taken his girlfriend, who was only fourteen at the time, and the pair of them had gone on a killing spree.

"Not Carol," I whispered. "He said *Caril.* He was looking for his girlfriend, *Caril Ann.*"

Every kid in Lincoln knew at least part of the story. It had been romanticized in movies and such in the years since it had occurred. For some, it had all the earmarks of the James Dean sort of 50's rock and roll, horribly tragic love story. Most Lincolnites, however, didn't see the romance. They saw the horror.

Charlie and Caril were poor, wrong-side-of-the-tracks kids in Lincoln. They'd been dating for a while before everything went terribly, terribly wrong. Caril's mother, stepfather and baby half-sister were Charlie's first victims found by the police in January of 1958.

When Caril came home from school that day, Charlie was in her house, and her family was nowhere to be found. According to Caril, Charlie insisted that her family had been kidnapped, and if they notified the police, they would be killed.

For the next week, the two holed up in Caril's house, staving off the queries of concerned friends and family with a note on the door that read, *"Stay Away. Every Body is Sick With The Flue."* Caril's grandmother wasn't convinced, and being highly suspicious of Charlie, she went to the police.

That's when Charlie and Caril took off. The bodies of Caril's mom, step-dad and baby sister were discovered, horribly murdered, in the out-buildings behind their home. From then, and for the next week, Lincoln

Nebraska was an armed camp, with everyone in town terrified that they'd be next.

The two of them had taken off in Charlie's black, 1949 Ford and gone to Bennett, a small town on the south edge of Lincoln. There, they killed an old man, and soon after, a young couple who'd stopped to give them help with their car, which had gotten stuck in the mud. After those murders, inexplicably, they came back to Lincoln, where they killed a wealthy man, his wife, and their housekeeper and hid out in his fancy house in the Sheridan neighborhood. After a day or so there, they stole the man's Packard and headed west for Wyoming. One more man was killed during their flight before they were finally caught, and yet another victim was found after all was said and done.

At the very end, Caril fled to the police, claiming she had no knowledge of her family's demise, and holding to the story that she'd been Charlie's captive the entire time.

The court of public opinion had gone hard on them both, but in the end, Charlie was convicted of one of the murders, and sentenced to death in the electric chair. Caril became the youngest female in US history to be tried for first-degree murder. She too was found guilty and sentenced to life in prison. She spent more than 17 years in a women's correctional facility before finally being paroled in 1976. She maintained her innocence throughout.

Nobody really knew the truth about what had transpired between the two. Some people held fast to the idea that 14-year-old Caril had been a willing participant, that she was every bit as evil and damaged as Charlie. Other people were just as sure she was a victim, not just kidnapped by Charlie, but totally messed up in the head by her relationship with him.

Fourteen years old was the same age as my sister, Mallory.

"It's really him? This is the ghost in the school?" I asked. My guts felt cold, and I was suddenly afraid I was going to barf. Back at school, with my lemon squeezie and my cocky confidence I had been scared, but not like this. This was different.

To me, Starkweather was a monster. A real, human, monster. Not only did he kill people, and lots of them, in totally gruesome ways, but he turned somebody he was supposed to be in love with into something awful too. Regardless of whether he turned her into a killer, or just a horrible pawn, without him, she'd probably have been a pretty normal kid. Possibly a miserably unhappy kid, but at fourteen, who isn't miserably unhappy at least part of the time?

"I believe so," Mr. Rakow replied solemnly.

"Cool....!" whispered David.

"Not cool!" I exclaimed, whacking his arm. "I mean, yeah, cool as a scary bedtime story, but not cool like this!"

"Angie's right. If Charlie's even half as dangerous in spirit form as he was when he was alive, it's going to be bad," Mr. Rakow cautioned.

While the three of us went back and forth about it, Jen wandered off again. I kept one eye on her. She seemed a bit off to me like she was watching, or maybe listening for something. When she froze, hands up in a *wait...just wait* motion, I started for her.

She stood motionless, a few rows away from Charlie's headstone. A sunbeam arrowed through a gap in the tree beside her, lighting her up like she was on stage.

"Jen? You ok?"

Silence. I quickened my pace.

"Jenny?"

I was totally focused on her and didn't notice the car that pulled in and parked behind Mr. Rakow's.

"Jen, what is it? What's wrong?" I got to the spot where she stood, stock still. I reached out to touch her, then changed my mind and walked around so I could see her face. Her eyes were focused at some point a million miles away. Her hands were still up in that, *wait* gesture. A quick glance told me she was breathing normally and nothing appeared to be horribly wrong ... also I had no clue what was going on in her head, so I waited.

A car door slammed. I caught movement out of the corner of my eye. Jenny remained frozen in place. A familiar voice behind me said, "It's okay, baby. Speak. Tell us what you see."

Jen's face suddenly became super animated. First with curiosity, then concern, then alarm. I felt warm hands squeeze my shoulders, and Lorraine's voice again, soft and gentle, "It's okay, honey. Speak. Let it out."

Jenny gasped, her words tumbled out in a rush. "The circle! It's broken! Watch out!!" Her expression became fearful, her gaze still distant.

"What is it, honey?" Her mom urged, still calmly, like this was not weird at all. "What should we look out for?"

"The circle! It's broken! Car! Fire! It's burning!! Mr. Rakow! NO! Run! David run!" Her voice had ratcheted up, her hands now gesturing like she was directing us which way to go.

"Ok, honey. It's okay. Your words have been heard. We heed your words." Lorraine's hands were still on my shoulders, but I could tell, it was Jen she wanted to be comforting. For reasons known only to her, she held back. Jenny quieted, her arms still upraised. "Is there more, Jenny hon? We're here. We're listening."

Jenny didn't look at us; her eyes still focused on some faraway point. Abruptly she spun around and knelt at a nearby gravestone. "Granny. Yes, that's it. Go with Granny. She knows how to take care of everything." Then she sighed a peaceful, happy sound and flopped down in the grass.

Jen's mom came around me and settled to the grass by her side. She put her arm around her daughter, who blinked like she was coming awake.

Jen scowled. "What happened? Why am I sitting here?" She looked at her mom. "And why are you here? Aren't you supposed to be at work?"

Jen's mom smiled. "Honey, we need to talk."

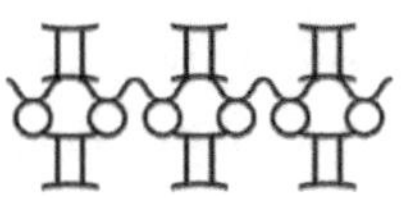

Twenty minutes later, David and I were back at Mr. Rakow's house. Jen had gone in her mom's car, and Mr. Rakow, although he seemed to have an inkling what was going on, refused to answer any of the million questions David and I hurled at him.

We waited impatiently for Jen and her mom to pull up out front. Once they did, Jen hopped out of the car like nothing in the world was wrong. She bounded up the front steps, returned David's proffered high five, took one look at my anxious face and put an arm around me.

"Guess what, guys! I'm a prophet!" She guided me through the screen door, David and Lorraine bringing up the rear. She squeezed my tense shoulders and whispered in my ear, "Don't worry, it's all good, and there might even be more cool news, too."

Mr. Rakow had set the iced tea and glasses out, but nobody touched them.

"We have a lot of ground to cover," said Mr. Rakow cautiously. "Lorraine?" he looked at Jen's mom. "Ladies first?"

She steepled her fingers together and stared at them for a breath or two, trying to decide where to begin. "What Jenny said is true. What you guys just saw was a prophecy." We all stared at her expectantly and waited, while she chose her next words.

"Some people have a little extra…" she paused.

"Power?" I asked "Gift?"

She smiled at me. "Something like that," she answered. "I learned about it from my grandmother. Everyone thought she was a little touched, but I was always fascinated by her stories. She's the one who taught me about the magic that can come with the sign under which we're born."

"Are you talking about, like, horoscopes? asked

David dubiously. "I thought that stuff was just made up. My horoscope in the newspaper is totally bogus."

"That is absolutely correct, my boy." Jen's mom replied with a nearly inaudible sigh. "The horoscopes in the newspaper are nothing you need to worry about. What my granny worked with was a whole lot more complex than that, and I'm not going to give you all a three-hour lecture right now, either."

She put a finger up and looked directly at me. "Yes, Angie girl, I know you're going to want to devour every bit of information you can about this, and I have a trunk full of books at home that I will be delighted to share with you, but for right now I'm going to try for the short and sweet version."

I settled back, secure in the knowledge that my future contained a trunk full of bookish delights, and listened carefully...and yes, I pulled my ubiquitous notebook and pen from my pocket and poised myself to jot down notes. I was, and remain, a slave to my curiosity.

"Jenny was born on what's called a Cusp. It's the dividing line between two astrological signs. She was born on the border between Sagittarius and Capricorn, which is known as the Cusp of Prophecy. Now, that on its own doesn't gift her with extra sight, but since she was born into a family of Practitioners on my side and prescient dreamers on her dad's side, it happens that she has the gift. It often materializes about this time, in the early teens."

"So, what Jenny saw in the graveyard was the future?" I asked. If our future contained burning cars and fleeing, I was pretty sure I wanted Jen to change the channel and show us a different future.

Jen's mom smiled at me. "Prophecy is a tricky business, Angie girl. The signs we see aren't always absolute or precise," she said.

"What use is it, then?" David asked. He glanced at Jen, who shot him an inscrutable look. "I mean," he hurried to explain, "I'm not saying it's not amazing and cool, but if we aren't sure how accurate it is, how are we supposed to use it?"

Mr. Rakow put a hand on David's arm. "I know what you're saying, buddy, but I've dealt with prophecies once or twice before. In my experience, even if they're not exact, they can still be useful."

"How so?" David pushed.

"They can give us a general sense of what we're facing. If Jenny can remember any details of what she saw, it could tell us some things, like a location, or maybe things we would be able to prepare for."

"So, in this case, we need what? Fire extinguishers? Running shoes?" David was serious, and I thought he made good sense.

Jenny's mom groaned. "Angie girl, write those down in your notebook, please? We're going to have plenty of magical and supernatural concerns; it's good to have someone thinking about the practical things, too!"

"Mom, you should tell Ang and David the rest of what you told me in the car!"

"But wait! There's more!" joked David in his TV announcer voice. "For just the cost of postage, you too could be the proud owner of…" he paused. "What'll it be, Johnny?"

"For you, today…" Jen's mom's eyes sparkled. David made her laugh as much as any of us. "The Cusp of Energy!"

"What's that?" David asked. I was pretty sure he'd been hoping for the Ginsu knives.

"That's you," Jenny's mom replied with a smile. "And you, my dear," she looked at me. "You were born on the Cusp of Beauty."

Jenny smiled conspiratorially. David leaped up and began doing jumping jacks. I blushed hotly.

"And what does all that mean?" asked Mr. Rakow, chucking an ice cube at David, which David deftly caught and redirected back into his tea glass with perfect aim. *Swish.* Didn't even spill the tea. I rolled my eyes.

"You might be able to guess some of the Energy Cusp's gifts," chuckled Jen's mom. "Fun loving, strong, physically and mentally agile…"

David was now executing a handstand, close to, but not touching Mr. Rakow's refrigerator.

"Mentally?" The jibe came from Jen and me simultaneously.

"Hey!" David crowed, still upside down. "I resemble that remark!"

"And you, Angie girl," she continued. "Don't get all self-conscious about that name; it's not exactly what you think. The Virgo/Libra Cusp tends to grace people with a really lovely balance between the intellectual and the artistic."

"So you, Miss Brainy Musician, fit right in!" Jen poked me in the side as she spoke.

Relief cooled my cheeks a bit. "Ok, I can probably see that. But what does it mean for us? Is it why we can see the beasties? Do we have any extra power, like Jenny?"

"That, Angie girl, is something I'm still trying to figure out."

"And how, exactly, Miss Lorraine, are you going about doing that?" Mr. Rakow asked, a glint in his eye like he already knew the answer.

Jen's mom shot him a look, but Jenny jumped in before she could speak.

"Magic!" she said firmly.

The conversation continued for another hour until David's rumbling stomach reminded us all that we were starving and had places to be for supper. I won't recreate the entire conversation, as it was plagued with interruptions, questions, and one major disagreement. The long and the short of it, as gleaned from my little notebook later, is as follows:

Despite the three of us being born on Zodiac Cusps, it didn't automatically follow that we'd all be gifted with any special power, like Jen. But, it was something Jen's mom was delving into. She had more access, of course, to their own family history than David's or mine, but she was working on it, among her other extra-curricular projects. It was evidently a fascinating and frustrating search.

The disagreement was mainly between Lorraine and Mr. Rakow, and it revolved around what to do about Charlie's ghost.

Mom was sure that there was a magical solution, and Mr. Rakow was unconvinced. He believed, given the rage and violence Starkweather exhibited during his life, his ghost could be powerful enough to defy traditional enchantments.

"Lorraine, look at what he's already done! The physical manifestation of the car alone gives us a glimpse of how much power he's capable of. Let alone trying to turn Miss Angie into a dartboard!" Jen's mom nodded and shook her head at the same time. Until that conversation, I didn't even know that was a thing you could do. Adults. Go figure.

We broke for dinner, but not before Jon called, looking for us. Jenny, David and I filed out of Mr. Rakow's house, electing to walk the few blocks home, rather than riding in the car with Jen's mom, who had decided to get carry-out rather than cook.

"Whatcha thinkin', Angie?" David asked a block or so later, peering at my face. I shook myself out of my reverie.

"I hardly know where to start!"

Jen was staring at me intently. I knew what she wanted. This was supposed to be my thing. I was the one who took complicated problems and broke them down into bite-sized chunks. But this was stretching my skills, big time.

"Guys, I feel like we need a rulebook, and there isn't such a thing. We know that freaky messed-up shit exists. We know some of it's dangerous, and we know that somehow the three of us plus Mr. Rakow and Jen's mom are not only able to see it but are somehow better equipped to deal with it."

David started bopping around, posing like a body-builder. Jen thwacked him in the back of the head, which slowed him down a little.

"But I'm worried that we're getting ahead of ourselves."

"How do you mean, Ang?" David asked, pausing briefly mid-pose.

"Well, we know this ghost is dangerous and powerful. We're pretty sure that tornado thing awakened him but we don't know anything about how or why *that* happened, or who, if anybody, is behind it. We don't know what Charlie's ghost might do. Is it here just to stir up mindless trouble? Or did whatever raised it up have some evil plan?"

"Evil plan?" Jen almost laughed, but not quite.

"Yeah, you know, in the movies, the villain always has some plan for world domination!"

"You think Charlie is like, some sort of soldier of the Evil Empire?" David asked, only half-joking.

"I don't know! I wish I did! … I think." I frowned. "What I do know is that the three of us are looking at trying to figure out a way to get Charlie's ghost out of the school, and we have tools we don't really know how to use, and information we're sure is incomplete. Working out with Mr. Rakow, getting stronger and smarter about fighting is a good start, but there's a whole lot more we need to figure out."

"But, that's what Mr. Rakow and Jen's mom are here for, right?" David asked.

I looked at Jen, confirming that she was thinking along the same lines I was.

"Yes and no. After listening to them just now, it seems like they're on different sides of the problem, or at least of different minds about the solution, anyway."

"Yeah, Mr. Rakow wants a physical fight. Mom wants a magical one," Jen said, thoughtfully. "What do you think, Ang?" Her eyes, enormous and green, were troubled.

"I think," I paused. "I think I don't know. And I want to … no, we *need* to know. We need to know more about ghosts, about what they can do, about magic, and about your prophecy gig, Jen. I don't see how we can possibly go up against this thing without knowing more. I think we got totally lucky last time, against whatever possessed Mitch. I think we're a little bit better prepared now than we were then, but we have our work cut out for us, trying to figure out exactly how we're supposed to get rid of Charlie's ghost!"

We were nearly to Jen's house, and from where we stood, I could see down the street to mine. Both cars were in the driveway, which meant my mom was home from her class and my dad would have supper about ready. I needed to hightail it.

"What's the plan, Ang?" David asked.

I turned to them and decided fast. "For now, we find out all we can. Jenny, bug your mom more. See what you can learn about your dad's family and how your prophecy thing works." She nodded back, decisively.

"David, You're on Charlie detail. Past and present. Find out all you can about him and watch for signs at school. Is he just going to rage around and destroy things? Or is he smarter than that? We know he's looking for Caril, but she's long gone from Lincoln, Mr. Rakow said. How is he going to track her down? Can he? Is he stuck at the school? Or is he already out hunting for her?"

"On it!" David saluted.

"What are you going to do, Ang?" Jen asked.

"I'm going to learn all I can about magic, see if your Mom is right about using magic against Charlie, or if Mr. Rakow is right and we need to focus on physical, what do you call it, mundane stuff."

"How are you going to do that?"

"I'm not for sure, but I know where I'm going to start."

Jenny winked at David, and they both grinned. "To

the library!" they crowed, fists upraised.

"It's like you know me." I laughed.

"Angie!" my sister's voice floated down the block. I glanced and caught her wave from my front porch. "Get your butt home! Dinner's ready!"

"Gotta jam, guys. See you tomorrow!"

David caught us up in the goofy, ever-evolving handshake he'd made up for the three of us. He looked like he was about to add yet another move to it when my sister yelled again.

I grinned and turned to race down the block.

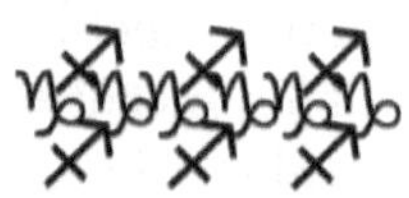

The next few weeks were a blur. The three of us were sneaking around, trying to root out intel about all kinds of crazy, killer, ghosty magic stuff without raising the concerns of any of our fine, upstanding Midwestern elders, or in David's case, getting caught lurking around off-limits areas of the school without getting busted by the 'Dean of Discipline.' Besides which, our classes were consistently getting tougher and requiring more reading, more homework, and much to my dismay, pop quizzes. I was of the mindset that pop quizzes were all the solid evidence needed as proof of the existence of an Evil Empire.

Jen was having better luck, to begin with, because she had her mom to talk to, but even that was limited, partly because Lorraine was reluctant to let Jon in on the whole story. I think she was afraid he'd want in on the action, and that was something she seemed unwilling to allow.

She did try to include him in learning about their family history because there was at least some chance of him exhibiting abilities in the soothsaying department.

Jen's mom said the women of the family more often had it, but Jen and Jon were twins, and that put an unknown element into the mix.

As it happened, Jon wasn't particularly interested in family history, or if he was, it took a distant second place to pick-up ball and arcade games.

Jenny, however, was entranced by what she was discovering. She hadn't known much about her dad's side of the family before now, so it was all new to her.

I was a little jealous, to be honest. Jen didn't seem to be having any trouble at all spending hours going through boxes of old letters and pictures her Aunt Sonya brought over, while still keeping up with her classwork. In fact, somehow, she even found time to audition for the all-school winter play.

I, on the other hand, felt like I was barely keeping afloat. I had a novel to read for Advanced English, Algebra was kinda kicking my butt, and on top of that, our conductor was attempting to put together a quartet, and was adamant that he needed me, the only oboist, to be a part of it.

Plus, I wasn't making any good progress finding reliable sources on magic. The school library was zero help, and the public library wasn't much better. My favorite librarian did the best she could for me, but beyond a book about Paganism by an author called Adler, I wasn't getting much in the way of useful information and my anxiety levels were rising to new levels.

It was David's investigations that were netting us the most relevant results, which turned out to also be the most disturbing. And that wasn't the only disturbing thing happening.

Right around then, Jen found out she'd made callbacks for one of the lead roles in the play. David and I were waiting for her to come out after seventh period to let us know if she'd gotten it, when a commotion started near the bike racks. A fight had broken out. A dozen or more kids had formed a circle around the combatants and were chanting that age-old chant of rapt onlookers every-where - FIGHT! FIGHT! FIGHT!

Last year, I'd have shrunk back from anything resembling trouble, but this time I followed David's lead and waded into the crowd. When we saw who was fighting, we were floored.

Circling one another in the center of the crowd of kids was a boy named Brian. He was skinny and pale, with stringy blonde hair, and he played second chair violin. Not your typical brawler. More bizarre yet, he seemed to be the one who had picked the fight.

I caught sight of his best friend, a French horn player named Dan who we'd known since kindergarten. He was holding Brian's violin case and looked both shocked and fascinated by what was unfolding.

The target of Brian's fury was a boy - a ninth grader. A kid who not only had at least six inches and twenty pounds on Brian but who, it was rumored, drank beer on the weekends and already had the first of what I felt sure would be many homemade tattoos.

My jaw dropped. I made my way quickly over to Dan. "What's going on?" I hissed.

Dan's face was scrunched up with worry.

"I don't know! Brian doesn't even know that guy, and all of a sudden, he just went off! He handed me his stuff and ran over to the kid and hit him!"

"Little dude socked Rodney right in the jaw!" crowed a boy to my left. He sounded impressed.

As we watched, flabbergasted, Brian started yelling, "Damn bully! I can't stand bullies!" and he waded in again, both fists flying.

Rodney, who at first had looked just as baffled as everyone else, got a mean look in his eye and put up his fists, eying Brian like he was a piece of meat that needed tenderizing.

Before either of them could connect, a figure zoomed in from behind Rodney. It was David! He came in low, underneath Brian's flailing fists, caught him around the waist and pushed him out of Rodney's reach.

One of David's big football friends, Jason, took over and pinned Brian's arms to his sides. David whirled around to face Rodney.

David addressed the older kid in a remarkably calm, collected voice, "It's all cool man. We got this. No need for any trouble."

Rodney, still flustered, shouted, "Little shit just came out of no place and sucker punched me!"

"Yeah, man. I know." David commiserated. "We got this now. It's cool."

I don't know if it was David's quick action and soothing words, or the fact that three more football players had come to stand by him, but Rodney decided not to press the issue further.

He shrugged his shoulders and turned to walk away. Shaking his head, he growled at David, "Keep your shit-bag little friend away from me, Owens, or next time, he's toast!" He shouldered a couple of his friends who had come to watch, and the three of them ambled away, digging crumpled packs of cigarettes out of their jean jacket pockets and deliberately not looking back.

Dan and I ran over to where Brian was still being restrained. His face was red, and snot was running from his nose. He looked near tears. David was speaking to him in a low voice as if he were quieting an agitated animal.

"It's cool man. It's all over. Chill out. It's ok now."

"What happened, Brian?" I asked. "What did Rodney do to you?"

Brian shook his head once, then again like flies were buzzing around his ears. David gave Jason a look, and the big guy loosened his grip on Brian's arms.

"He called me some name..." Brian's voice sounded lost, confused.

Dan looked surprised. "When?"

"Just then! I heard him say it! Called me ... something ..." Brian's eyes glazed over again, and Jason responded, adjusting his grip, in case Brian started freaking out again. But Brian stayed still.

"He called me … a peckerwood?" It came out almost in a whisper. He looked around, his eyes lit on me, and he frowned, confused. "What's a peckerwood?"

Nobody knew what to say.

David and I marshaled a couple more friends to help Dan get Brian home. We watched them until they turned the corner, and then I asked David, "What do you think that was all about?"

He glanced around to see if anyone was nearby before he spoke. "It was about Charlie."

"You're sure?"

"Absolutely."

"Crap."

We waited around another ten minutes for Jenny and finally took off and headed over to Mr. Rakow's.

✳ ✳ ✳

"Mr. Rakow, there was a fight after school today, and it's not the first one," David began.

"Oh yeah? What are you thinking?" he asked, eyeing David speculatively.

"I wasn't sure before today, but now I am. This has to have something to do with Charlie."

"Charlie's starting fights?"

"He's doing something! I overheard some teachers talking yesterday, they said the number of fights already this year is almost equal to what they had the last two years, total."

"What made you sure it was Charlie?" Mr. Rakow asked, curious.

"Because just now, Brian picked a fight with a kid who could have, and still might, pulverize him. And when we broke it up…"

"When *you* broke it up," I interjected. I was still pretty impressed with how he'd managed it. David tipped an imaginary hat my way.

"Afterwards, he was out of it. Like he was on drugs or something. And when we asked him what Rodney did to him, he said he bullied him and called him a peckerwood."

David had filled me in on some of these details on the walk over, and I was eager to see what Mr. Rakow was going to make of it. Apparently, it was well documented that in Charlie's childhood, he was a bully's wet dream. He was small, poor, bowlegged and red-haired. According to what David had found out already, the slang, 'Redheaded Peckerwood' was both prison lingo and small-town redneck dialect, so I'm sure it was an epithet Charlie heard more than once in his short lifetime.

Mr. Rakow sighed heavily. "Dammit."

"Are you thinking," I asked, trying to put it all together, "that Charlie's ghost is projecting his pain from back in school on other kids?"

It sure seems to fit, Miss Angie. You said your friend Brian wasn't ever bullied by the fella he attacked?"

"Not that we or Brian's best friend Dan ever knew about," I said. "We can try talking to Brian again later, once he's feeling better."

"That's a good idea. He may be able to give you some more clues, like what was going on when it got started."

"Yeah, something that might help us figure out if Charlie's ghost is picking people at random or if something is setting him off." I mused.

"That's it. Smart girl. Keep up the brainwork." He adjusted the toothpick that was forever clenched in his teeth. "Where's Miss Jenny this fine afternoon?"

"She made callbacks for the play. She's probably doing something with those theater kids." I didn't realize how aggravated I was feeling about her blowing us off until those sour words came out of my mouth and David and Mr. Rakow looked at me with expressions of mild surprise. I blanched. "Sorry. I guess I'm a little peeved."

"I'm sure she has a good reason for whatever is going on," Mr. Rakow reassured me, his tone soothing.

"No doubt," I replied, trying to keep my tone civil.

"Oh, Miss Angie, that reminds me. I have a line on those books that might help us out."

"Books?" My attention was instantly diverted.

"Yes. Lorraine and I know a woman who has a collection of books about magic. She's not been around for a while, but I got ahold of her granddaughter, Melanie. She lives near Lincoln. You'll have to get permission from your folks to drive out there. This weekend, maybe?"

"Yes! I'll ask!"

"And what are we supposed to do about the kids fighting each other at school?" David asked.

"Watch. See if you can figure out if there are any common elements that set it up. Watch out for your friends, and especially one another. Stay safe. The sooner we can get this figured out and get Charlie's ghost to move on or piss off or whatever his ghostly ass needs to do, the better off we'll all be."

"Yeah, before someone gets really hurt," I said.

"Or really dead," David agreed.

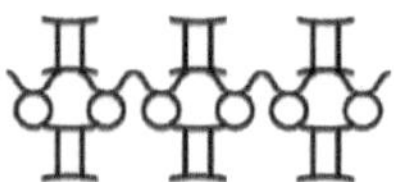

I told my folks that David, Jenny and I were invited to go with Mr. Rakow and Jen's mom to the Pumpkin Patch. These were annual fall attractions in and around Lincoln, part farm, part fair. They had games, sometimes rides for the little kids, and usually a corn maze. My folks were not big fans of this particular form of entertainment, so they were just as happy I'd be going with someone else.

I overheard them talking afterward. My dad asked my mom, "Is Lorraine dating Rakow?"

"I don't think so," my mom replied. "But they have been spending a lot of time together since Lorraine took on David while his mother recovers.

"How's Donna doing, by the way? We haven't been to see her for a couple of weeks."

"I dropped off some of those Krispy bars we made last Saturday, remember? Not much change. That accident really did a number on her."

"It certainly did, and she wasn't in the best of health, to begin with, was she?"

I couldn't hear my mom's response, but I figured she was shaking her head. Nobody had said so yet, but I didn't think David's mom would be coming home any time soon, if ever. That thought made me both sad and scared, so I pushed it away. As crazy complicated as attempting to use magic to banish a dangerous ghost was, it seemed the more solvable problem of the two.

It wound up being just me and Mr. Rakow on Saturday. Jenny was at play practice. The fall production was to be 'A Christmas Carol' and Jen, appropriately enough, had gotten the role of the Spirit of Christmas Future.

David had been recruited for the Cross-Country team. With his glass eye, the football coach had been reluctant to let him play, and he was decidedly unhappy about sitting on the bench. So, the two coaches had put their heads together and cooked up an alternative plan. I wasn't totally surprised that David went along with it; he'd always been good at running.

The problem was, between his and Jen's schedules, we weren't able to spend much time on the Charlie problem, and I was starting to get more than my usual amount of worried. Well, worried and a little pissed off that my friends were blowing me off, but I tried to squash that down, telling myself that it was all okay. All I had to do was more research, figure out a way for the three of us to effectively banish our homicidal ghost, and all would be well.

Charlie certainly wasn't slowing down any. Fights were becoming more and more frequent, and I was seeing that old black car around the school almost daily.

Mr. Rakow and I took off from his house in his old beat-up Nova. We headed south, just out of town; maybe a twenty-minute drive.

"So, who is this lady we're going to see?" I asked.

"She's the granddaughter of a woman I used to know when I was younger. It's her books I'm after, and Melanie, the granddaughter, is keeping care of them now."

"I'm sorry, is the grandma dead?" I asked, trying to remember if he'd told me that part earlier.

"Um, not exactly," he hesitated. "I believe she's traveling. I explained to Melanie what we needed, and she said she thought she could help."

We turned off the gravel road into the driveway of an old farmhouse, not unlike many others around here. The farmland itself was probably rented out, but the house still stood in good shape. I saw a barn out behind the place and a fenced grassy area. I wondered if they had horses.

We opened the car doors and were greeted by a couple of raggedy looking barn cats and a very happy medium-sized dog of no particular breed. A youngish woman stepped out of the screen door wearing faded jeans and a Fleetwood Mac concert tee. Her brown hair hung down her back in a long braid.

"Hey Rakow," she greeted us. "Hey, kid."

"Mel, this is Miss Angie, the one I told you about who is interested in books." I smiled shyly. She stepped off the porch and came toward me. I thought she was going to shake my hand, so I stuck mine out. She ignored it and instead grasped me by the shoulders and examined me closely like I was some new species of butterfly.

I submitted meekly to the examination, wondering what she was seeing. Whatever it was, she seemed satisfied.

"This is the scholar," she said in a decided tone to Mr. Rakow. "Where are the others?"

"They had practice today. I'm sorry, I didn't realize you were expecting all three." Mr. Rakow seemed a little flustered.

"This will do, for now," Melanie replied simply. "However, Grandmother will want to see them all when she returns."

"Any idea when that will be?" Mr. Rakow asked as we made our way up the stairs and across the generous porch.

"No." She opened the screen door and ushered us inside. There was a living room to the left and a hallway immediately in front of us, running alongside the staircase. I could see the kitchen at the end of the hall. Sunlight streamed in on all sides from big open windows.

Melanie led us through the living room and into the connected dining room. She silently indicated that we should sit.

We sat.

The table was old, the chairs mismatched, and the hutch that ran the length of the wall was filled with fascinating things that had nothing to do with dishes or glassware. Behind the glass doors were books, jars, boxes, candles and things I couldn't immediately identify.

Everything in the room was meticulously clean and organized, but clearly worn and well used. A large leatherbound book lay closed on the table. The whole house was redolent with good, earthy smells and there was a sort of musical hum to the air, though I couldn't discern any source. There was no radio playing — in fact I didn't see any electronic devices at all.

Melanie took the seat at the foot of the table, nearest the living room and gazed at me a moment before she spoke. "Miss Angie, my grandmother has instructed me to share some information with you, but only if you can assure me that your need is great and that you are prepared to use what I tell you." She held up a hand, silencing Mr. Rakow before he could speak. "This is for the girl, Rakow. We are fully aware of your and Lorraine's credentials, and no, before you ask, vouching for her is not sufficient. It was enough to bring her this far, but now she must show us that she is ready to take this next step."

I wondered who "we" was, as there were just the three of us in the room, but I didn't ask. From her jeans pocket, she withdrew a yellow Bic lighter and lit a small candle that sat in a holder atop the old book. She didn't speak any magic words or do anything obvious, but the moment the flame was lit, the whole room felt different. The quality of the light changed, and the outside sounds were slightly muted. It was like we were all in a bubble.

"Talk to me. Tell me what you've learned about this ghost," Melanie instructed.

A test. Okay. I could do this. I sat up a little straighter in my chair and began. I told her about the Ouija board, and the tornado, about meeting up with the angry spirit in the music room at school, and how it had attacked me. I told her about the lemon squeezies, the black car, everything. Then I told her about the fights at school, specifically the one Brian had started, but I'd done some asking around since, and I laid out for her the details I'd learned about other altercations.

There had been no fewer than two fights a week since school had started, sometimes more. Repeated reports of bullying. Broken glasses, torn clothes, kids who had never been in trouble, like Brian, suddenly picking fights.

I told her about Jenny's vision, that she'd seen us making a circle and then it being broken so Charlie could rage through it, about us running and being blocked by a fire and the black car. I told her about what David had learned about Charlie, how he was bullied, how he'd bonded with Caril who didn't get along with her stepfather, and how she felt left out when her mom had a new baby with him.

I told her what Charlie and Caril had done, how many people had died, and how terrified and confused the town had been, and how unpredictable Charlie was.

She listened carefully throughout. I must have talked for more than half an hour, but although the candle dripped wax down its sides into the silver candle holder that separated it from the book, it never grew any shorter.

Then she asked about Mitch, and what had happened at the beginning of summer. I glanced at Mr. Rakow and he nodded, indicating that I should speak freely, so I did.

Once I'd finished, Melanie stayed silent for a time, staring into the candle's flame. Then, she turned to me. She spoke, but her voice sounded strange. It was different than before, older and sharper. She pinned me with her stare and asked, "What makes you think you are deserving enough, wise or powerful enough to use this knowledge, child?"

My heart stuttered and my hands shook. I answered without thinking. "I don't! I don't think I deserve it."

"Then why, child?"

"Because I have to! Because last time, when Mitch came, we - me and Jenny and David - we had to save each other, and we did it. And now, everybody at school is in danger, and we have to do it again. I don't know why, or how. I just know we have to try." My heart was racing and tears were threatening.

Everything about this was scary. I kept trying to keep a lid on my nerves by doing everything I thought I had to, in order to keep us all safe and alive, but I was mostly just whistling past the graveyard. Even with the three of us working as hard as we could together last time, we'd all ended up in the hospital, and David had lost his eye. I was trying desperately to counter that with training, knowledge, and thinking ahead, but inside, I felt like I was constantly battling my fear. Like it was a huge bear loose in my house, and whatever I did to stay in control, it was still a huge bear, and I was just a dorky twelve-year-old kid with an oboe and a library card.

Melanie's face softened. Her voice returned to its usual tone when she said, "All right, Miss Angie. It's all right. You did well." She nodded to the candle before blowing it out and setting it carefully aside. Then she opened the book.

I sniffed and rubbed at my face with the back of my hand. It wasn't an ordinary book, not that I'd really expected it to be. The pages were old and heavy, and the words were handwritten, not printed.

I was torn between wanting to pore over every page, and not wanting to touch it at all. I sat quietly and waited. Melanie delicately flipped through until she found what she was looking for. The page she stopped on had a title written in a language I couldn't read and hoped I wouldn't be expected to. I was still shaky from the last test.

"The binding spell you will need is one that is, at its heart, familiar to Lorraine. What is different in this case is that it will need to be both stronger and cleverer than usual. You're right, Rakow, in thinking that Charlie isn't a regular ghost. Typically, for a ghost to manifest anything in this plane is difficult to the point of impossibility. He has shown us, with his physical and psychic attacks, with the manifestation of the car, with the sheer amount of disturbance that he's been able to accomplish, that he is being fueled by a power beyond his own."

"You mean he has help?" Mr. Rakow asked, his tone dire.

"Either help, or he has access to a power source. That is not yet clear, and it is part of the reason Grandmother is traveling right now. But she feels, and I agree, that you three have become some kind of nexus for power and that with help and guidance, it's you three; the scholar, the prophet, and the warrior, who can counter this dark power in this time.

Lorraine has sufficient magical skill to produce the initial spell. I will provide you with the tools you need to strengthen it. Rakow, your understanding of the darkness will enable them to put the spell into action around this spirit's interference. And have no doubt, he will try to interfere.

"He believes he is bound to Caril, and it may be that her soul is attached to his in a way that might strengthen his power, or in fact, may limit it, we cannot know for sure. But what we do know, is that he cannot be permitted to find her. He must be bound while he is still attached to this place, this school.

"The binding will come first. He must be drawn into the circle and contained. From there he must be banished entirely from this plane. The salt normally used for bindings and protection will be insufficient. Your prophet has shown us this." She reached into the china hutch and drew out a small white bag tied with a string. "This will enhance your salt circle so that it may withstand his added power."

I saw Mr. Rakow cock an eyebrow at the word, *may*, but he kept silent.

She placed the bag carefully on the table and consulted the book again. "Lorraine will need to make new candles for the spell. I'll include a list of items she'll use for the making. She drew a sheet of paper from another drawer in the hutch and wrote several items on it in charcoal pencil. Then she rolled it up and tied it with a bit of blue string. She lay this by the bag of salt, then opened another of the hutch's many compartments. She looked at me pointedly as she drew out a large leather-bound volume and a long, thin box with hinges on the long side.

She handed me the book, first. "This is an excellent text," she said. "It was compiled in the early part of the century, and encompasses, among other things, the grimoires of many generations of witches and wizards whose lives spanned the last several hundred years. A witch called Phyllida Peterson compiled it. It will be an excellent starting point for you. Grandmother said you were to be allowed to borrow it for as long as you needed. I'm sure you will have many questions, which you may save until she returns."

I reluctantly set the book aside, telling myself silently that there would be plenty of time later to absorb it. I was also super curious about the Grandmother but now didn't seem the best time to ask. I kept still and listened.

Melanie lay the long box out on the table between us. "Grandmother began preparing this in the spring, apparently even before you confronted your goblin. She doesn't tell me everything, but she has obviously been preparing for your visit." She winked at me.

Goblin? Mitch? I resisted the urge to flip open the book she'd given me immediately and start looking things up. The Grandmother had known? I wasn't sure if this was glad tidings, or just creepy. I smiled at her. I think.

She opened the box and inside lay three simple necklaces on leather thongs. Each was ornamented with a single charm - a stone - bound inside a delicate wire cage. She pointed to them in turn. "For the prophet," she pointed to the necklace on the left. A red stone glinted from inside the latticed cage. "For the warrior," she pointed to the one on the right with a green stone. "And for the scholar." The necklace in the center had a deep blue stone.

Something about the necklaces captured all of my focus. I was so drawn by the tiny glimmers of color peeking through the fine gauge wire that I missed what Melanie said next. I came back to reality when she closed the box and latched it. I flushed and looked up guiltily. She had a serious look on her face.

"Please keep them all together until you're with the others. I know they're compelling, do you think you can wait until you can give them to your friends? It's very important that you put them on all at the same time."

"I can," I replied. Any twinge of impatience I felt was easily canceled out by the exciting thought of presenting them to my best friends.

"Excellent." She lowered the lid on the box and set it next to the other items. "There's one final thing.

Grandmother has requested that you make a choice."

"A choice?" Mr. Rakow spoke for the first time in a while. I glanced over in surprise at his tone. I couldn't quite identify it … not shock, but pride? I wasn't sure.

"Come with me, Miss Angie." I stood and followed Melanie into the kitchen. She led me to a cabinet full of small drawers.

At first glance, I thought it was a card catalog, like at the library, but it was slightly different. I sought out the word when I got home. It took a while, these were the pre-Google days, mind you, but I found it! Melanie stood in front of the apothecary cabinet, motioning for me to join her.

Once I did, I realized that this was the source of the musical sound I'd been feeling like a low hum in the base of my skull since we arrived. I listened hard, trying to identify the song. It was a little sweet, a little sad, and a lot powerful. Melanie spoke again and I shook myself back into the real world, if that's where we were.

"I'm sorry, what did you say?"

She smiled understandingly and said, "Choose a drawer."

I looked at the cabinet. Some of the drawers were tiny, some bigger. Four rows of five, three rows of four, one row of three. Each was unique, a different pull, a different pattern of paint, it was a fascinating piece of cabinetry. I could have stood and gazed at it for hours.

"Choose a drawer," Melanie repeated.

"How do I choose?" I asked, feeling in my bones that this was something important I ought not fail.

"Choose the one that speaks to you," she instructed patiently.

I studied the drawers a moment longer, but there really was no question. One of them was definitely speaking to me. Well, not speaking, exactly. More like singing. It was one of the smaller ones, near the top on the left. The pull was silver and shaped like a heart, but I'd recognized that the heart was made of two musical symbols, a bass

clef, and an upside down treble clef. When I reached my
hand toward it, a note sounded clearly in my head; the G
above middle C.

I glanced at Melanie, and, reassured by her smile and
nod, I opened the little drawer.

"Go ahead, Angie, see what the cabinet has for you."

I dipped my fingers inside and drew out a pin, like a
stick pin for a hat or a lapel. My Grandmarsons had some
in her jewelry box. This one was topped with a tiny
flower with petals in graduated shades of purple, palest
on the inside and darker on the edges of the petals, with a
tiny white stone in the center. It was old, and very pretty,
but better than that, even after I'd taken it out of the
drawer, it continued to hum the same note in my hand.

"It's beautiful," I breathed. I held my hand open and
showed her and Mr. Rakow.

"What kind of flower is that?" Mr. Rakow asked. "It
looks like the ones my mother used to call heart's-ease."
Melanie just shrugged. I'd have to look it up later

"What is it for?" I asked her. "I mean, I know it's a
hat pin, but it's more than that, isn't it?"

"Oh yes, indeed," she nodded, "but what that *more* is,
it's up to you to find out. The cupboard provides you
with what you need, but its gifts don't come with instructions." She stepped to a row of wooden hooks near the
back door and took down an old tote bag advertising
some bookstore. "Let's gather up your things so you can
get them safely home."

We filed out of the kitchen. I paused and gave the
apothecary cabinet one more look as I passed, and silently
whispered, *thank you.* In response, the little pin hummed
happily in my hand.

Melanie and Mr. Rakow had loaded our various gifts
into the tote bag, and Mr. Rakow carried it to the door.

"Thank you, Melanie."

"You're welcome, Angie. Good luck to you." She
pressed Mr. Rakow's hand. "I'm sure Grandmother will
be in touch as soon as she returns."

We drove off with me holding the tote bag on my lap, and the pin cradled in my hands. We stopped by Jenny's house. Jen's mom was home, but David and Jen were still at school. We showed Lorraine the list of ingredients from Melanie and she frowned.

"What's wrong?" I asked.

"Most of these things I can get my hands on fairly easily, but this," she pointed at a Latin name. I was guessing it was a plant. "*Hieracium Snowdniense*," she pronounced it carefully. "This one is going to take some doing. Even if I can get my hands on some seeds, this wants fresh petals, so I have to grow it. Damn." She shook her head and looked at Mr. Rakow. "I'm going to give Mel a call. Maybe she knows where I can lay my hands on some."

"When are David and Jen supposed to be home?" I asked. Jen's mom turned from the list, a distracted look on her face.

"Oh yes, I almost forgot, Angie girl. Jenny called and said she was going over to Stephanie's house to practice lines after rehearsal. David was going to have dinner with Jason. He should be home by 8:00 or 8:30."

"Oh." I glanced at the clock on the stove. 6:45. Damn. "Ok, well, I guess I'll walk over to the library. My folks won't be home for another hour."

"Do you want a ride?" Mr. Rakow offered.

"Nah, thanks. I'll walk." I tucked the book and the box containing the necklaces into my backpack and headed out.

Ten minutes later I was curled up in my favorite corner of our neighborhood library, pretending to read. Jeanne, my favorite librarian strolled by, adding some books to a display. "Hey, Angie! Everything okay? You look a little blue."

I smiled up at her ruefully. "Yeah, I just had some good news to tell my friends, but it has to wait because they're *too busy* right now."

"Oh wow, what a bummer." She arranged another

book on the display. "You know, I love good news."

I smiled and shook my head. "I would if I could, but you know…"

"Oh, *that* kind of good news. I get it."

"Wait, you know what? I almost forgot, there is something I need to ask you about!"

"Oh yeah? Hit me." She came over and perched near me on the window seat.

"It's this." I pulled the hat pin out of my pocket. "Do you know what flower this is?"

She peered at it closely. "I think so, but hang on. Let's do this right." She bustled off to the non-fiction section and returned with a book that sported big color pictures of different kinds of plants. We spent a pleasant few minutes debating about petal color and configuration before deciding it was from the viola family, with names that ranged from Johnny Jump-Up to Heart's Ease to Pansy to Love-in-Idleness.

"Say!" Jeanne remembered suddenly. "I think Shakespeare talks about these little guys," she popped up again and came back with a thick volume of Shakespeare's Annotated Plays. She flipped to the back and ran her finger along the index until she found what she was looking for. "Yes! Here it is, it's from Midsummer Night's Dream." She flipped a few more pages and started reading to me.

"Yet mark'd I where the bolt of Cupid fell,
It fell upon a little western flower,
Before milk--white, now purple with love's wound,
And maidens call it love-in-idleness."

I thought about that quote for a minute. "So, Cupid's arrow made it bleed?"

"Yes," she responded. "You could say that."

"So much for true love being a happy thing, huh?" I grinned a little and rolled my eyes.

"Well, yes … and no." She pushed her red hair back behind her ear and smiled her crooked smile at me. "He says here in the same play that 'the course of true love never did run smooth.' I think that applies to all kinds of love, not just romantic love. Friends, families, all of us. We always struggle with disagreements and hurts. It's all part of the big picture."

"You think so?" I hadn't really considered this before, and I wasn't sure I liked it. "Pain is just part of love, part of friendship?"

"I do. It stinks, but look how beautiful the outcome can be," she said, pointing at my pin. "The flower wouldn't be half as pretty if it stayed all white, would it? Look at how much more interesting and beautiful it is with the colors."

I smiled politely and filed that thought away for later, but honestly right that minute, I was pretty mad at my friends, and not really in the mood to be philosophical about it. I was trying not to feel that way, but it wasn't working.

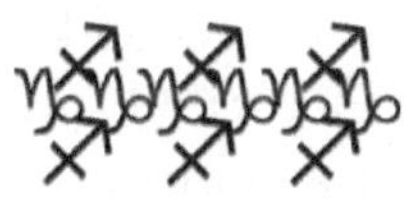

I'm pretty sure it was shortly after that trip to the library when my nightmares started. Well, no, not nightmares exactly. In order to have a nightmare, you have to be asleep. It was hard to tell for sure sometimes, but looking back on it, I think I was mostly awake when they would occur. I'm also quite sure there's more about it I've forgotten than what I've been able to recall.

I remember snippets of lying in bed during that time, half-frozen in that semi-conscious 3:00 am way, staring up at the ceiling and trying really hard to figure out what had caught my attention. Was it a sound? A movement? My room would be dark, but the streetlight outside always cast a faint glow around the edges of my curtains.

Then the cold would begin to seep through me, and

the whispers would start. Words I was just on the verge
of making out, like a scratch-off puzzle coming to light.
Then the emotions would flood in, rocketing through my
heart - fear, sadness, anger, terror, longing. I couldn't separate cause or effect, reality or dream, just the sense of being swept around and around in a whirlpool of feeling.

Then a voice, scratchy and harsh, *Come to me. I need
you.*

I would fall back to sleep, shivering under the covers.
In the mornings, I would wake with no recollection of the
dreams but for an unsettled feeling that something or
someone was doing me wrong.

It stayed with me, that feeling. A pinprick of anger,
like a stone in my shoe.

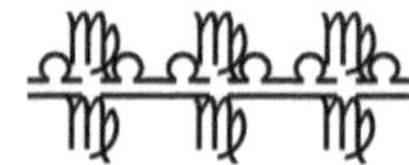

For the rest of September and half of October, I
don't think I was together with both Jenny and David for
more than five minutes at a time. Certainly not long
enough to have any kind of serious conversation, and absolutely not enough time for all of us to put those necklaces on at the same time, as I was instructed.

To be totally honest, I was busy too. Mr. Quick, my
orchestra teacher, had managed to put together a pretty
fun quartet, and we were rehearsing twice a week, getting
ready for the pre-winter break concert. Since I was newest
with my instrument, and everyone else had been playing
theirs for at least three years, I was absolutely and totally
determined not to suck.

Jen's mom had finally gotten hold of the flower
seeds she needed, from a mail-order place in Wales, and
was meticulously working with them to ensure we had a
sufficient quantity on hand for the spells we needed. Mr.
Rakow had even helped her construct a little greenhouse

in the backyard.

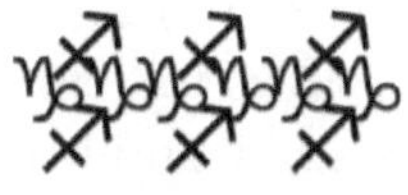

"I can't believe they're having play practices both be-fore *and* after school!" I grumped at David as we made our way to school without Jenny. Again. I'd had another short night's sleep, laced with half-remembered dreams. It was beginning to get to me, although at the time I didn't realize how much.

"Yeah, I think she got roped into building sets as well as being in the cast."

"Indentured servitude. Gotta love it. We have a huge Spanish test coming up next week, too!"

David looked at me curiously "Are you mad about something?"

I paused and eyed him. He sallied ahead, bravely. "You're practically stomping your feet, Ang."

I grimaced, forcing myself to chill out and think … and walk like a normal person. "Yeah, kinda. I guess."

"So, spill it," he instructed. David wasn't usually, let's-talk-about-our-feelings guy, but he was good at call-ing us all out on our bullshit.

It was at this point that I tossed any attempts at keeping my cool and spilled it. "Dammit! I feel like we're all a million miles apart, and I'm freaking out about Char-lie! It's like we're in this holding pattern, I know we're waiting for Jen's mom to get the spell stuff ready and all that, but we're just farting around, and nobody's talking, and kids are getting beat up every freaking day, I just, I don't know…" I trailed off.

I still hadn't mentioned the necklaces to either of them. I knew it was stupid and snarky. I think I believed those represented my last tiny piece of control over this mess, and I felt like I needed to hang on to it.

"Are you worried about the spell working?" David asked.

I sighed. "Yes and no. I mean, I totally trust Jen's mom, but this is new to her, too, and she's having to use ingredients she's never used, and Mr. Rakow still thinks we need more than just the spell, and the fights, I mean, did you see Jackie and Dana yesterday after third period? They've been best friends since second grade, and yesterday Jackie gave Dana a black eye and Jackie ended up with a broken wrist! And I'm swamped with school stuff, and you're swamped with cross country stuff and Jen is always busy with the play and her stupid theater friends!"

I stopped when David put his hand on my shoulder.

"Sorry," I muttered, head down. "I know I'm flipping out."

"Yeah, but that's what you do, and it usually works for you," he replied in a calm tone.

"What do you mean?" I grouched.

"I mean, that's like, the way you think. You think about all the stuff you have to do, and just before you have to use everything you know, like on a test or whatever, then you have your freakout. Then you chill out, and you're good. You're like that thing Jen's mom uses on the stove for the tea."

"What, the tea kettle?" I asked, scowling.

"Yeah. Just before the water is ready, it screams. That's how you know the water is boiling."

"Great. I'm a tea kettle."

"Haha, no. But you are building up a head of steam."

"So, what should I do about it?"

"What am I? Your shrink?"

"Apparently so!" I snapped.

He shrugged and continued walking. "I think you should talk to Jen."

"But that's just the thing! She's never around!"

"You're the smart one, Angie. Figure something out." The first bell rang just then, and we sprinted the half-block to the front doors. "Talk to her!" he hollered, turning down the hall to his locker.

Damn. Was I the one being the jerk? Sure, Jen was busy with stuff, but so was I. Was I making an effort? Was she? Oh, to Hell with it. She had rehearsal tonight, as usual. I'd been trying to get in extra practice time, but I could skip it once and lurk around the stage. Surely there would be a minute here or there where we could talk.

If she even cared, said a pissy little voice in my head. *Stupid play. I bet she didn't care. I bet she wanted to hang out with Stephanie and all those other theater kids. I bet she…*

That's when I tripped over the shoelace I was one thousand percent sure I'd double-knotted that morning and went sprawling.

Fortunately, the bell was about to ring, and so the number of people who might have seen me face-plant on the floor in front of my math class was smaller than it could have been.

Unfortunately, the one person who just *had* to be there was Stephanie, the beautiful, perfect, talented theater girl. The one who was helping Jen run lines all the time, even when there wasn't a scheduled practice. She looked down at me, flipped her perfectly feathered hair over her shoulder … and freaking laughed.

I saw red. I mean, literally, it was like somebody had dropped a bloody haze over my vision. I leaped to my feet, fists clenched, ready to sprint down the hallway and smash that shit-eating smirk right off her perfect f…

"Hey, Ang … Angie? You dropped your books." A hand on my arm, "Angie?"

I spun around, my eyes blazing to see … Dennis. Pale, short, Dennis, with glasses that were as thick as my thumb. Dennis. Holding out my math book and looking puzzled.

"Angie? Are you okay?

"I …" I took a deep breath and let it out. The red mist started to fade. "Yeah, sorry Dennis. Thank you."

"No problem," he smiled shyly. "C'mon. We're already late."

"Yeah, right. Thanks." I dusted myself off and shuffled into class, careful of my shoelace until I could sit down and retie it. What the hell had just happened?

I leaned over to tie my lace, and ice-cold air made the skin on my neck prickle, then it got a million times freakier. A finger of ice ran very deliberately down my spine, paused just above the waistline of my jeans, circumscribed a circle and then disappeared.

My gut dropped, like a hardcore Orient Express roller-coaster at Worlds of Fun drop. I wasn't sure if I was going to poop my pants, barf, or curl up like a three-year-old and sob. What I was sure of, was that it had been Charlie.

Mrs. Jackson was passing out worksheets. She paused at my desk and looked down at me. "Are you okay, Angie? You're white as a sheet. Do you need to go to the nurse?"

"No - I … I'm okay. Thanks." I took my worksheet and dug around in my backpack for my mechanical pencil. My fingers touched something unfamiliar. I drew it out.

It was a little plastic doll, maybe three inches high with a bald head except for a little curl on the forehead. It looked old and creepy. I stared at it for a second and then dropped it back in the bag. I shuddered and zipped my bag shut hard. Whatever it was, I was sure it too had something to do with Charlie.

Omigod. I was *so* done with creepy. Even math sounded good in comparison. I vowed to show the thing to Jen's mom and Mr. Rakow later. Until then, that backpack was staying fricking closed.

I made it through the rest of the day and instead of

my usual forty-five extra practice minutes after school, I
headed for the drama room, next to the auditorium.
There were groups of kids sitting around on the floor in
the hallway, huddled together over scripts. I almost
tripped over a pair of feet sticking out nearly to the center
of the hall.

"Whoops! Sorry!" I mumbled, blushing.

"Hey! Angie!" the person attached to the feet said.
"How's it going? I had to look at him twice before I recognized Alan. We'd had the same teacher in third and
fourth grade, but then he moved or something. I didn't
remember seeing him all last year. He'd grown about a
foot and had something vaguely resembling a mustache
going on, or maybe it was just a trick of the light.

"Alan! Hey! I didn't know you were back!"

"Yeah, my dad's construction job in Des Moines got
finished and my mom wanted to come back - so here I
am! Good to see you!"

"You too!"

"I haven't seen you around here, are you working on
the play?"

"No, just looking for Jenny. Is she in there?" I asked,
nodding toward the drama classroom.

"I think I saw her painting sets - that way," he
pointed to an unmarked door behind him.

"Thanks, Alan. Maybe I'll see you later."

"Yeah! Later!" He went back to the scene he was rehearsing with a skinny, black-haired girl I didn't recog-
nize. I offered her an awkward smile and pushed the
wooden door.

It opened into semi-darkness. I looked around to get
my bearings and realized I was backstage. I heard voices
off to my left.

"Who taught you to paint, Heather? Jackson Pol-
lack?"

"Like, what does that mean?" responded a tart voice
I guessed belonged to Heather.

"It means, we're supposed to be painting this wall,

not doing some abstract splatter pattern on the floor!"

"Jeez, Michael. Who died and made you the boss of us?" asked another voice. I recognized Jenny's voice and that tone. "If you spent as much time painting as you did showing off your wicked knowledge of contemporary art, we'd be done by now."

Yep, that was Jen. Michael, whoever he was, stomped off in a huff.

"Like, what was he talking about, anyway?" came Heather's injured retort.

"Oh, nothing, just showing off. Do you have enough paint to finish that side, Heather?"
"What? Oh, fer sure, like, I think so. Omigod are we ever going to get done with this?" I ground my teeth. Thirty seconds of listening to her insipid tone had me on edge. I didn't know how Jen had the patience. I peeked around the corner and was surprised to see Jen looking directly at me almost like she'd expected me to show up right that second.

"Hey Jen," I said, hesitantly. It occurred to me that I might have wanted to rehearse this conversation in my head a few more times before just barging in. Oh well. I was here now, and like David said, Jen and I needed to talk. I took a breath and let it out.

She sighed. "Hey Ang."

I pushed down a surge of irritation and said, a little snarkily, "Sorry to bother you. I know you're busy…"

Heather interjected, "Like so totally busy, ohmigod!" and then continued to stare at us, mouth open. I knew her from around, but I'd never had any classes with her. I gave her a strained smile and wished with all my heart she'd go away.

She didn't.

"…but we have to work on that … group project. I have some new, um, books that might be helpful."

Heather's head bopped back to look at Jen, then at me, totally absorbed in the fascinating *ABC Afterschool Special* that was apparently this conversation. I ground my teeth together and put my hands on my hips. "So, do you think you might have some time to get together with us?" I spit out.

Jen's head fell. It was a dejected move like she was bearing the weight of the world. I looked at her, confused. I couldn't for the life of me figure out what her deal was. I was so full of frustration I wanted to scream and stamp my feet.

All the stupid anxiety-ridden fears I'd been pushing aside since school started bubbled up in my heart; she didn't want to be friends any longer, I'd done something horrible and stupid to make her mad, the thing with Charlie wasn't important, she was going to dump us for her new theater friends, she was … I was …

Then, calmly, without looking up, Jen said, "Careful where you step, Heather, there's a can of paint right behind you. Then Jen carefully lay her brush down on the lid of the can she'd been using, got to her feet, wiped her hands on her jeans and lunged straight for me.

She must have been watching the football guys doing their drills or something. She hit me low and hard, and before I had time to react, she'd knocked me ass over teakettle and there was an explosion of sound and flying sparks.

Heather screamed and leaped backward, one foot landing squarely in the can of paint right behind her. She fell. Paint sprayed everywhere.

There was a collective gasp and a thundering of footsteps as everyone in the vicinity ran to see what had happened.

I peeked out from my prone position underneath Jen to see that the exact space I'd occupied seconds ago was now home to a several-hundred-pound stage light that had inexplicably fallen from the scaffolding above and crashed to the floor. If I'd been standing there, I'd have been crushed.

Jen propped herself up on one elbow and eyed me.

"So, that prophecy thing," I ventured.

"Yes, that," she replied in an even, almost expressionless tone.

"Getting kinda intense, is it?"

"You could say that."

"Well, shit-fire."

Jen smiled then, her regular smile. Her before-all-this-craziness-started smile.

I grinned up at her. "Thanks for saving my ass."

"Any time." She booped my nose once, and then we were mobbed.

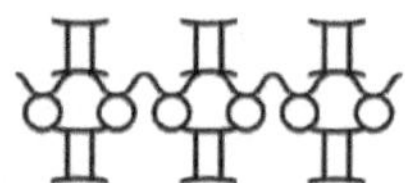

They ended up sending Jen to walk me home. That is *after* I was given a thorough prodding by the school nurse and pronounced only shaken up. We were strongly cautioned to take care on the way home and informed in no uncertain terms that our parents would be given a full report.

Jen glanced at the clock on the wall and indicated that we needed to get moving. I was in no mood to question her at this point.

As we made our way down the halls and out of the building, Jen started talking. Everything she'd been dealing with, it all just spilled out. It had started the night after we went to the cemetery with dreams, some of them really horrible. Trying to figure those out, what elements were prophetic and what was simply the product of her own wacky wonderful subconscious became a full-time thing pretty fast.

Her mom had promised several times to try to track down Jen's other grandma, but she hadn't had any luck, and since *she* was so absorbed in trying to get our spell and all its details straight, Jen had been trying to deal with it the best she could alone.

I felt horrible. I felt bad for doubting her, for being mad at her, for not just freaking asking her what was going on, and for missing it entirely. Plus, I felt bad because Jenny was feeling bad, and had been doing it all by herself, without any help from either me or David.

"Why didn't you say anything? Even if I couldn't have helped, I could have maybe *not* spent the last two months acting like a whiney baby and thinking you didn't like us anymore!"

"I know. I don't know," she replied. "It was all so totally out of the blue, you know? I didn't know what to think, or how to ask for help." Her face was sad and resigned, but maybe a little relieved too. I hoped so, anyway.

"I guess it just seemed like you and David were handling everything ok, and I was the only one who wasn't. I was embarrassed."

"Oh, sure, I get it. Like, a few extra trips to the library and choosing track over football are such MONU-MENTAL COPING TASKS. Like, *totally* comparable to discovering you have superhuman powers. Yep. it's all clear now." I stared at her.

She smiled. "It's a good thing you love me even when I'm being a moron."

"Yes, yes, it's all true," I replied. "Now, tell me oh vision-questy one, why are we going this way?"

"Because David is about to need a hand," she replied calmly. "You game?" she asked, challenge sparkling in her eye.

"I am if you are," I grinned, tightening the straps on my backpack.

"Let's go!" She pushed open the heavy fire door and jogged out into the bright afternoon sunshine.

"What do we need to do?" I asked, easily keeping pace with Jen's long stride despite the fact that I had to take three to her two.

"You know Frankie Madsen?"

"Um…" I searched my brain. "Short guy, stringy hair, hangs out with Bill somebody, he runs cross country, too, right?"

"Right. He's going to twist his ankle crossing the street by the park. He's going to sprain the hell out of it. David won't notice in time, but Charlie will."

"In the black car," I finished. It wasn't a question. Charlie would be like a tiger, just waiting to pounce on somebody weak and injured.

"Hit and run, but if David's timing is off by even a few seconds, they're both going to get hurt, maybe killed."

I could see the Cross-Country runners approaching the intersection already. I scanned them, trying to spot David or Frankie amid the group of runners. They were all wearing their team t-shirts, a uniform blue and silver, and it was hard to tell anybody apart. We were still three-quarters of a block away when I recognized David's dark hair and pointed.

"Frankie is the last runner. We need to get David's attention before he gets too far from the street."

"If we hurry," I puffed, "can't we save Frankie's ankle, too?"

She threw me a wink. "Let's change things!"

We broke into a sprint. The kids in the front of the pack looked up, startled from their tired, downward stares. We dodged around them in the grass. I didn't even think we were within earshot yet, but Jen's voice, strong from many years practice hollering at Jon to get his butt home for supper, proved me wrong.

"David! David Owens!" He was approaching the street, looking both ways. "David! Heads up!" she shouted. My ears rang, but it worked. He looked up. "Stop! Stay there!"

He cocked his head, confused, but did so still jogging in place. That's when I spotted Frankie, coming up behind David, preparing to cross.

It wasn't a busy street at all. It was hardly even a

street, really. It was about four blocks on the edge of a residential neighborhood, with houses on one side, and the park on the other. The coaches specifically routed kids this way because it was safer. Once they crossed this last street, they were in the park, and then on school grounds. It was the last place you'd expect to see a black, 1949 Ford, missing its front grille, appear out of thin air, already screaming along at 40 plus miles an hour.

The math didn't even compute. The car couldn't be going that fast - there simply wasn't enough space for it to accelerate. Yet, there it was.

There was something both terrifyingly real and yet unreal about the car. The sunshine glinted off heavy Detroit steel and thick glass, but then got lost in a black, smoky mist that curled out from underneath the body and trailed backward like a wake.

I remember thinking at the time there was something vaguely Tolkien-esque about it, and years later when I saw the Nazgul on horseback chasing down the Hobbits in the first of Jackson's *Lord of the Rings* movies, I had to leave the theater and do some deep breathing in the bathroom.

I don't know what David saw in our gestures, or heard in Jen's voice, but he figured it out immediately. Jen and I skidded to a halt at the sidewalk. Everyone was safely across, except for one. Bringing up the rear of the pack, running at a solid, steady pace straight toward the street, was Frankie.

He was tired but determined. He was looking down, not up, or side to side like he should have been approaching a street because right there nobody ever bothered.

And Charlie knew it. Somehow, he knew it. He bore down, the missing grille looking like the maw of some hellish beast

"Stop Frankie!" Jen bellowed. David turned, crouched, and tackled the unsuspecting kid to the ground. They sprawled into the grass bare inches from the curb. The Ford zoomed past, close enough to blow hot wind and gravel into Frankie's surprised face. I saw his eyes go from pissed to panicked in a flash.

For a second, I thought we were home free, and then Charlie cranked the wheel. The Ford spun. I was years away from driving at that point, but even I knew if you were going that fast in an old heavy car with crappy balding tires, there was no way you could spin on a dime like that without skidding or maybe even flipping the car.

Apparently, Charlie and his Ford were not subject to the same laws of physics the rest of us were. He spun the car like it was a tiny souped-up sports car with precision everything.

If I could have breathed, I would have screamed, but the only place that my cry sounded was the inside of my head. I was useless.

It was all David. When he'd tackled Frankie, he hadn't stopped his motion. Rather than allowing them to come to a stop at the very edge of the curb, he'd held onto Frankie and rolled. He rolled him over and over along the edge of the curb in the direction Charlie had come from, using his own speed against him.

No matter what means of defiance of the laws of nature Charlie had, there was a limit. He could speed, he could spin like an evil ballerina, but he wasn't quite able to completely reverse his trajectory on the spot.

David kept Frankie rolling until they reached the edge of the first driveway on the block, and then in a show of brute force, he scrambled to his feet, hauling Frankie up and dragging him up the driveway toward the house.

The Ford had stopped. The spin had landed its snout pointed back toward the boys. It paused a second, as if evaluating its options, and then the engine revved.

My heart nearly stopped. David and Frankie were pinned between the Ford, and the mess of cars and bikes parked in the driveway they'd scuttled up to. Their only escape route was through the house, had the door been conveniently open, which, of course, it wasn't.

David was scrambling, trying to pull Frankie up. From the way was Frankie was grimacing and holding his ankle, we hadn't managed to change that.

Charlie revved the engine again, and then from nowhere, a figure appeared, standing firmly between the boys and the Ford.

The figure, a woman, shimmered into view, almost solid, but still a little hazy around the edges. Like a person in an old-timey photograph who hadn't managed to stand completely still during the exposure.

She was older, maybe in her sixties or early seventies, but with a straight spine and a firm look. She wore a long coat and an old-fashioned hat. Sort of a Jackie O. look, but plainer.

She stepped firmly forward and shook a raised finger at the menacing car, as though she were scolding. Her face was a little fuzzy and unclear, but I could tell she was speaking.

Jen seized my shoulder, keeping me planted on the park side of the street. The sound of the figure's voice emerged, like the sound on our old TV used to, low at first, then warming. It caught up with her mid-sentence.

"... you won't! You will harm no more children this day! Git! Go on with you! Back to Hell where you came from!" Her old lady voice cracked as she shouted, and she made a shooing motion with her hands.

The Ford ... wobbled? Like it was losing its hold on the air around it. She shoo'd it again and it was as if she commanded a strong wind to obey her - blowing the Ford and Charlie away like smoke from birthday candles. A third wave of her hands and a whoosh. Charlie and the Ford broke into smoke and just ... dissipated.

My mouth hung open. Jen loosened her grip on my shoulder and we took a step forward. The woman caught sight of our movement, and stared straight at us, blue eyes snapping fiercely.

"You!" she pointed at Jen. "You, Prophet. You must speak your words! Belay your fear and speak! And you!"

She pointed right at me. "Don't be a fool! You will need to power of the Triad to banish this monster. I can disrupt the current, but only the Triad's power can send him back for good!"

Even as she spoke, she was fading - her blue-green coat transforming into blue-green smoke before our eyes. Her words were fading too, draining away. I strained to hear her before she disappeared completely.

"Use the tools you were given…" and she was gone.

Jen and I sprinted across the street to the boys. Jen got her shoulder under Frankie's other arm and she and David hauled him upright. Carefully they hopped him across the street.

"Where did the car go?" he mumbled. "Jerk didn't even stop, did he? Ugh. I must have hit my head, I didn't even see him go." He turned blurrily to David. "Thanks, man. I would have run right in front of him if you hadn't stopped me."

"Yeah, sorry about your ankle, man," said David, glancing at me and Jen over Frankie's head. It seemed clear that Frankie hadn't seen exactly what had happened. I shrugged and looked at the retreating line of runners who had continued on up the hill through the park like nothing had happened.

"Yeah, this sucks. I hope it's not too bad, the meet is next week." He tried to put a little weight on it and grimaced in pain.

"Don't push it, Frankie," I advised. "Let's get you inside and get some ice on it. The coach should be able to tell how bad it is."

We wrangled him back up the hill to the gym door and let David and one of the assistant coaches take him inside from there. Jen and I figured a second visit to the school nurse by the two of us this afternoon would raise too many eyebrows.

We made a plan to meet up after dinner and headed home.

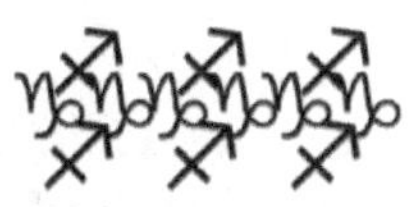

It was close to 8:30 before I could come up with an excuse to break free from homemade pizza night and run down the street to Jen's. Mom had given me a whopping thirty minutes to do whatever 'mega important' thing I had to do and get my butt home, so I ran instead of walking, the long box Melanie had given me thumping against my leg inside the bag where I'd secured it.

Jen and David were waiting for me at the bottom of the driveway. Once they spotted me coming, they set out and we met at the grassy space that ran the center of the block. We headed for our 'clubhouse.'

It wasn't a house, just a spot midway down the no-man's-land between the houses where some trees grew in an almost perfect circle. We had dragged chunks of wood and some other handy junk inside to make seats. The sun was down already, but the moon was nearly full, casting enough light through the branches that we could see pretty clearly for the moment.

I'd explained on the phone earlier that I'd been given these items at Melanie's house the day I went with Mr. Rakow.

"I think this might be the 'Triad' the ghost or apparition or whatever she was, was talking about. At least, I think it might be related."

"What did she say again?" David asked. He'd been behind her, with his hands full of Frankie, and hadn't been able to hear the words she'd spoken to me and Jen.

"She called Jenny *Prophet* told her to *speak*," Jen looked down at her hands. I put one of mine on hers. "Specifically, to *belay her fear, and speak.*"

"Belay?" David prompted. "You're the one with the vocab super-powers here, not me."

"Belay is like, stop it or quit it. She needs to quit being afraid of the dreams and visions and tell us about them when they happen. I'm not sure why that makes a difference, but I think it's kinda like the naming thing." David frowned and cocked his head at me. I continued, "There's power in names, in *speaking* names aloud. I think it might be related to that."

"Like, if Jen says the words out loud, they, like, come true?"

"I'm not sure. I'm still trying to figure that out. The book Melanie loaned me is part diary, part textbook. I'm still working my way through it. It's not," I paused for the right description. "It's not like a traditional textbook with a table of contents and an index. I'm having to read it forward, backward and upside down in order to follow it properly."

"So then, what did our ghosty lady say to you?" David asked.

"She said, I needed to use the tools I was given. She said she could disrupt the current, but only the power of the Triad could banish him for good."

"Again with the vocab," David grumbled. "Can't ghosts and magicky types just use regular words?"

"There is just too much weirdness in that sentence to even start with, and Angie has like, twenty-one minutes left before she has to bail," Jen interrupted.

"A triad is just three things," I explained quickly.

"So, what three things is she talking about?" David pressed.

"I think maybe she's talking about these." I pulled the box Melanie had given me out of my bag and set it on my knees. I flipped it open and for a second, my breath was taken away. The moonlight on the stones should have barely illuminated them, but they were much brighter than that.

"Whoa," David's tone was hushed.

"Amazing," breathed Jen.

"She said we were supposed to put them on all at the same time."

"Which is which?" David asked.

"I think I know," Jen said. They're our birthstones, aren't they?"

"Yes," I considered. "They are that at the very least."

Her hand reached and paused, hovering over the red stone. I glanced at David who was frowning in concentration. "Is mine, green? It … it feels like…" he trailed off.

I smiled and nodded my head, holding my hand over the blue stone. In unspoken agreement we lifted our respective necklaces from the box, and, eyes locked on one another, put them over our heads at the same time.

For a second, I felt a buzzing vibration in my chest where the stone lay, encased in its little wire cage. Almost like it was a living thing. From the expressions on Jen's and David's faces, I suspected they were feeling something too. David held the stone out in one hand, frowning at it. Jen had let hers lay where it fell, just below the neckline of her ring-neck tee, and her hand settled lightly over it, a faint red light shining between her long fingers.

Our eyes met again and I felt a physical … tugging sensation. It pulled me bodily forward a few inches. I threw my arms out to my sides to keep my balance just as the others did the same thing, and without a thought or a plan, we were suddenly gripping each other's hands.

The light I'd first mistaken as a reflection of the moonlight was, in fact, emanating directly from the stones. By forming the circle, that became entirely obvious, as delicate beams of light shot out from each and met, forming a solid, bright triangle.

I couldn't look away. My heart raced and my grip on my friends' hands tightened. The lights - red, blue and green began to swirl around and around, then grew large enough to encompass us within itself.

There was music in the dance of light. I couldn't tell if it played just inside me or not, but it filled my ears and my heart with a heavy, solemn joy. I had no idea how it was happening, or what was behind it all, but it felt very, very right. Somehow, being here in this place, the three of us together, was the most perfectly right thing for us to do.

The lights shone, and the music thrummed, gathering speed and power until I felt sure it would all explode like a firework, but instead, it turned inward, into us. For a moment, all three of us were suffused with a shimmering aura of colored light. Jenny's green eyes and David's brown ones glowed, and then with a little pop, the light was gone. Soaked into each of us.

I looked down at my legs sticking out of my shorts, half expecting to still see red, green and blue shining from my skin, but all I saw was my regular legs, glowing pale in the moonlight. I looked back up at my friends and realized we were all grinning like idiots.

Jen squeezed my hand and one side, and David's on the other.

"I don't have any idea what that was, Ang, but I feel like I could run a four-minute mile right now!" she said, her voice serious and happy at the same time.

"No doubt!" I exclaimed. "I feel like I could fly!" We looked over at David who seemed a little uncomfortable. "You okay?" I asked concerned.

His stomach let out a massively audible rumble. He grinned sheepishly. "I am freaking starving."

We burst into laughter. Very faintly I heard my name being called.

"Crap! That's my sister. I gotta go. See you guys to-morrow?"

"For sure. Can you do the paper route with us in the morning?"

I nodded. Tomorrow was Saturday, I was sure my folks wouldn't mind. "Five thirty?"

Jenny nodded and beaming at me, let go of my hand. "Now, fly!"

I flew. Or it sure felt like it for the long block home. For the first time since school started, I felt right. The long weeks of uncertainty and doubt were gone. Not gone, exactly, but behind me. Like that light had come inside me and cleaned house.

Jen's preoccupation with her newfound power seemed totally understandable to me now. Of course, she'd been freaked out! Who wouldn't! And David's concerns about sports - his fears of not finding his way again with only one eye? Why couldn't I have realized it before? My friends hadn't been dismissing or ignoring me. In fact, we needed each other more than ever, and now, thanks to a little magical kick in the butts, we all knew it.

Whatever that light had been, it left me with a clear understanding of my friends, what they needed from me, and what I needed from them. There was no way we could be separated. We were solid. We were balanced. We were the Triad. That was us.

I arrived at my front door, barely even out of breath. My sister stood inside the door, the inevitable paperback in her left hand, her index finger marking her page, her right hand on the porch light switch.

"You're late. Mom's gonna be pissed."

"I'm like, thirty seconds late. Mom will probably forgive me."

"Only if you finish putting away the pots and pans from supper!" Mom called from the TV room.

"Okay, mom!" I called, winking at my sister, who scowled.

"What's that?" she asked, pointing her book at my necklace. "Who gave you that? Do you have a boyfriend?" she demanded in an accusatory tone.

"Nope. It was a gift from one of Jenny's mom's friends. She gave Jen and David one too."

"David's wearing necklaces now?" she jeered. "Next thing you know he'll be getting his ear pierced!"

"Whatever." I shrugged past her and headed for my room to drop my bag before finishing up in the kitchen. I hurried because there was one other thing I knew now that I needed to do. Even my sister's dumb commentary wasn't enough to damage my good mood. I carefully hung the bag on a hook in my closet and trotted into the kitchen, humming a tune under my breath.

I slipped out the front door the next morning as soon as I spotted Jen and David coming down the block. I made sure my house key was in my jeans pocket before quietly closing the door behind me. I trotted across the street and we headed down the hill to Jen's paper corner.

"Mom is almost ready for a trial run on her spell," Jen filled me in as we walked.

"How is that going to work?" I asked. "How will she know if it works without using it on a real ghost?

"Solid point, Ang," David mumbled. He looked like his body was more awake than his brain.

"She and Mr. Rakow think they have a plan for that. They've been doing a bunch of research on local ghosts, and they think they have one to try the spell out on."

Since it was Saturday, the papers were pretty light. We split them equally into the front and back of Jen's carrying bag and she folded and rubber banded as we walked. My eyes focused briefly on a photo of some local event in the paper. It was a group of people, one of whom was holding a curly-haired baby. My sleepy brain toyed with that image for a second before the lights went on.

"Oh my god, you guys. I haven't told you about yesterday morning at school!" I watched David's face as he mentally ticked back over yesterday's events - the backstage light, Frankie, the necklaces…

"What, there's more?? You really pack a day full, don't you, Angie?"

"Yep, that's me! Arranging the world just so, to keep things exciting. Ha! If only."

"So, what happened?" Jen asked, tossing a paper expertly so it landed squarely on the Landis's welcome mat.

I relayed the story, starting with walking to school with David and our conversation that spurred me to quit being an idiot and talk to Jenny. When I got to the part about feeling all ragey at Stephanie, Jen looked thoughtful.

"You think Charlie had hold of your feelings there?" she asked.

"I'm sure of it," I said grimly. "Whatcha thinking?"

"I'm wondering, do you think he *only* had you there at the school? Or do you think he's been influencing your feelings about us this whole time?"

I considered this, little half-forgotten snippets of my nightmares tickling at my consciousness. "Do I think he's capable of doing both, the rage fit thing he's been putting on other kids to start fights, as well as a more subtle whammy?"

She nodded.

I shuddered. "Maybe? The rage thing seems more like Charlie, doesn't it?"

"Or maybe the subtle stuff is just a side effect of his presence, not necessarily a deliberate thing," David suggested.

Jen and I looked at him pointedly.

"What? I can't be all intuitive with the magical mumbo-jumbo sometimes?" Jen high fived him.

"It sure seems plausible," I shuddered. The idea of Charlie in my head at all was super creepy, whichever way you looked at it.

Jen sensed my mood, and asked quietly, "What else happened?"

I swallowed, goosebumps erupting on my arms as I recounted finding the doll in my backpack. I had pushed the whole thing to the back of my mind, just like I had the dreams, and with the events of the rest of the day, I didn't realize how much inner freakout that whole scene had caused me. I hadn't really processed it at all.

By then we were done with the route and on our way home. It was still early, sunrise was over an hour away. Jen had deftly detoured us toward the clubhouse while I was talking.

We shuffled into the secluded little grove. Jen dropped her newspaper bag and motioned for me to sit. She kept a hand on me the whole time, keeping me safe and connected. I looked up from my reverie and saw David peering at me with a weird expression on his face, part curiosity, part fierce protectiveness.

"What? I asked, already half dreading what he was going to say.

"What kind of doll was it?"

"What? Oh, one of those, old-fashioned plastic things, with the curl on the forehead."

"A Kewpie doll?"

"Yeah, why? What is it?"

David's expression was grim. "Charlie's first victim. The one they didn't connect until after everything was over with. Robert Colvert."

"He was killed *before* the killing spree in December?"

"What happened?" Jen's and my questions tumbled over each other.

"He worked at a gas station on Cornhusker Highway. Charlie went in one night and tried to get him to let him have some things on credit. Colvert refused. Charlie robbed the store and kidnapped Colvert. He drove him outside of town and murdered him." David shook his head in sadness and disgust. "Colvert's wife was pregnant, too. Their kid never knew her dad."

We digested that for a moment in silence.

"What is it that made you think of that?" Jen asked carefully.

David's mouth tightened into a grimace. "The doll. I've seen a few different versions of the story, one said he tried to buy a stuffed animal, but another said it was a Kewpie doll."

I paled, comprehension dawning. "A gift. He was trying to get a gift for Caril."

David nodded grimly.

Jenny all but growled, "If this lunatic has his eyes on you as some sick replacement for Caril, he's in for a world of hurt."

"Yeah," I said in a small, but firm voice. "Sorry, Charlie. I'm really not in the market for a barely literate, homicidal, already-dead boyfriend."

I need you. My subconscious cringed and pushed that figment of memory away.

David stayed quiet, but I saw the tension in him. *The warrior*, Melanie had called him. I could see it. Jen's hand tightened on my shoulder.

Unconsciously, my hand fluttered to my necklace. There were no two ways about it. This sucked, and my friends were awesome.

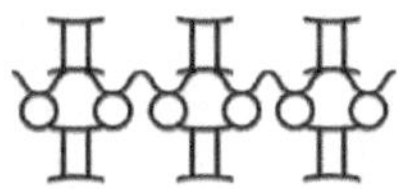

When we got back to Jenny's house, her mom's car was gone, and there was a note on the table. *Gone to test some ingredients with Mr. R. Will be back by 8:30. Help your-selves to cinnamon rolls.*

Jen tossed her newspaper stuff in the hall closet and the three of us started putzing around the kitchen. Pillsbury rolls dipped in butter and cinnamon sugar was one of our standard after-school snacks. Wholesome they were not, but dang they were tasty.

About the time we'd polished off the whole batch, Jen's mom and Mr. Rakow stumbled in, looking like they'd just survived some bizarre stormwind. Mom's hair was a spectacular mess, and every part of Mr. Rakow's face not protected by his glasses was coated with an unidentifiable mix of goop.

"What happened to you guys???" we demanded in chorus.

They took one look at one another's faces and burst into hysterical laughter. It took the better part of an hour to get the whole story out of them, between the laughter, the talking over each other, and one or the other of them running off for a wash.

It turned out, they'd gotten permission to attempt to banish a ghost from some guy's house. He was a friend of a friend of Mr. Rakow's, and he'd rented a house over near 63rd and Holdrege. He'd been surprised at how affordable the rent was until he'd moved in and the craziness had started - noises, cold spots, slamming doors, electricity going on and off. It had gotten to the point where he'd actually interacted with the ghost a couple of times. Nobody was sure of the how, when or who, but it was clear the ghost had unresolved issues about some lost love and remained seriously unhappy about the whole situation.

The guy had tried to get out of his lease, but the landlord was intractable and he was stuck. Mr. Rakow heard about it from their mutual friend and offered to step in and try to help.

Everything was going pretty smoothly, all the spell ingredients seemed to be working and they had the pissed off ghost contained, then they moved on to test #2. What if, like in Jenny's very first prophecy back at the cemetery, what if Charlie could use that demonic '49 Ford to shatter the protective circle, and dismantle the spell while it was in progress? The only way to test their plan was to deliberately break the circle.

Apparently, what happened was an extreme ghosty freakout in the kitchen of the dude's rental house. The goop coating Mr. Rakow was the contents of the kitchen cupboards; flour, sugar, breakfast cereal, and unfortunately for Mr. R, maple syrup. In the end, they'd succeeded in re-containing the ghost, and banishing him, but mostly because of the quick thinking of Gerry, the guy who lived there.

According to mom, who was telling the story between gasps of laughter, Gerry had learned a few things from his three months of interacting with the angry spirit. One of those was, the ghost had a real penchant for maudlin breakup songs due to his interminable heart-break.

"You're kidding, right? He what, serenaded the ghost?" Jen asked.

Jen's mom dissolved into laughter again. Mr. Rakow sat at the table, his hair wet from his attempts to bathe in the bathroom sink. "He cranked the stereo," Mr. Rakow said.

"What song?" David asked, eyes sparkling.

Mr. Rakow groaned.

"What? What was it?" I asked, trying to keep a straight face, a neat trick given that Lorraine, who was sitting across the table from me was absolutely unable to stop laughing. Tears streamed down her face, and she gasped for breath.

"Air Supply," Mr. Rakow sighed like it pained him to say it aloud.

"Let me guess…" Jen said, holding a hand up to David who looked like he was about to burst with laughter. She took a deep breath and started singing, "I'm all outta love…"

Mr. Rakow moaned. Lorraine and David exploded with laughter. Jen winked at me and grinned. Once the hilarity had died down, I asked, "So what happened?"

"The ghost stopped in its tracks. Started floating back and forth between the stereo speakers, moaning and wailing like a lost puppy." Mr. Rakow scrubbed at his face. "Gerry held him there in the living room while I snuck out the back door and sealed up a new, intact circle around the house. Once that was up, Lorraine was able to break her own circle in the kitchen, release the spell into the larger area and it worked! We bound the spirit and got the jerk banished!"

We celebrated the success with scrambled eggs and bacon. Then we spent the rest of the morning practicing making small personal-sized salt circles in the backyard and imbuing them with our will to make them close. Lorraine tested our circles by tossing handfuls of flower petals she'd enchanted to smell like poop at us. If we failed to seal the circles properly, we'd get a face full of ick.

David and I got the hang of it fairly quickly, and it only took a few more tries for Jen, with the added motivation of being pelted by poop petals from all sides, to get hers to seal up successfully.

An idea for a plan had started forming in my busy brain over the last weeks, and now that we knew Mom's spell would work, it was time to get busy implementing it. Knowing Charlie had an eye on me in particular only added fuel to my fire.

When I voiced my thoughts, Mr. Rakow immediately sat me down at the picnic table in the backyard and we started laying out our strategy. Jen and David popped back and forth into the house, bringing out pens, paper, toy soldiers, Legos, and Matchbox cars.

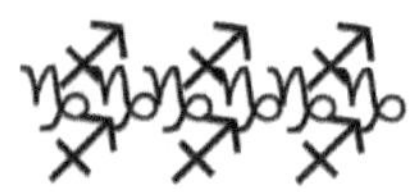

Jen's mom had been studying astral charts and had, perhaps unsurprisingly, lit upon Halloween as the most opportune time for us to act. That gave us just over two weeks to gather our supplies and figure out how we were going to break into the school on a Sunday night without getting caught.

The ongoing argument about whether Charlie or his demonic Ford would be vulnerable to physical attacks was compromised on, and we set to work creating tools and weapons both of the physical and the magical variety.

Most of the supplies we needed were reasonably easy to obtain if a bit odd. Mr. Rakow had an army buddy who had become a priest, so the gallon jugs of holy water created less of a problem than it might have. The trickiest issue ended up being how to get inside the school, and much to Mom's chagrin, that problem was solved neatly and almost professionally by Jennifer.

David and I were waiting for her as she strolled casually out of the school at about 3:25 on the Friday before Halloween. I had been doing my level best to keep my freakout to manageable proportions, but having to leave this bit until the last minute had just about done me in with anxiety.

Looking at her now, that casual stroll, I knew she'd succeeded, and every bit of my worry was smashed by fierce pride for my friend's accomplishment. Jen had managed to get herself called into the principal's office at the last minute on Friday afternoon. While being lectured in his office, she'd stolen his keys. We strolled coolly for a few blocks and got ourselves safely across 66th street before I broke down and demanded the details.

Jen shrugged and said "He tosses his keys on the little file cabinet by his desk when he walks into his office. When he lectures kids, he stands up and paces and looks out his window. She slipped into an eerily accurate impression of the man, *Back in my day, young ladies were polite and interested in learning, not disrupting classrooms! Blah blah blah...*

"Which one did you end up using?" David asked, grinning mischievously. The two of them had had endless discussions about which prank was most likely to get Jen into the principal's office, but out again without much lasting damage.

"Had everybody in Science say they were hearing a buzzing noise. By the end of the period, half the class was rolling around on the floor moaning, covering their ears."

"How did they know it was you?" I asked.

"I was the only one who didn't hear it," Jen said with a crooked smile.

I could picture the scene, everyone in class taking advantage of a dumb prank to kill the last hour of a Friday, and Jenny sitting in the back of the room, smiling like a satisfied cat. Mr. Bigham must have been going out of his mind.

"What if he realizes it was you who took his keys?" I asked.

"Nah, before he even got a chance to finish lecturing me, Tony and Todd and three other guys got rolled into the office for fighting in the gym. It was total chaos. Everyone was running in and out of his office. It could have been anybody."

I pinned her with a stare. "Was Charlie behind that fight? Or did you orchestrate that too?"

She winked at me, solemnly. I shook my head in awe. It never failed to amaze me how Jen could get other kids to do crazy stunts, and they'd come away from it feeling like they'd just managed the coolest thing on the planet. I'd seen her pull stuff like that a hundred times and I still couldn't figure out how she did it. She'd make a great General, or even Commander in Chief someday.

"Did you figure out a costume?" I asked David. We'd bowed to the fact that our best cover for approaching the school on Halloween night was to look like any other trick-or-treaters. It had proved an interesting challenge, to figure out what to wear that we could still run unencumbered in, plus carry the tools we needed to enact the spell and stop Charlie.

Jen had opted for the gray/green space jumpsuited Sigourney Weaver from Alien. Lorraine had incorporated a few 'witchy' details into her normal garb but drew the line at the pointy hat. My options were a little limited by the plan, but I'd tweaked things to make my costume more practical.

"Yeah, Mr. R had some army stuff that fits me," David shrugged.

"Put a headband on and you could be John Rambo," I joked. David rolled his eyes. It would take some time before that movie reached any sort of cult status. At that point, it had only been out a week and was still gaining steam. David and Jon had gotten Mr. Rakow to take them and had been only mildly impressed.

"Did you get your skirt issue figured out?" Jen asked me.

"Yeah, my mom wasn't happy about it, but she got my aunt to help and we got it altered."

"Cool. When are you coming over Sunday?"

"I'll probably be up early anyway, so I'll just come help with the route. Call me if anything comes up before then." Jen nodded. David drew us in for one more complicated handshake and we separated in front of my house. "We've got this, right guys?" I asked, feeling both anxious about what we were about to do, and so totally ready to have it over with.

"We so have this," David said, orchestrating the handshakes deftly.

"We are unstoppable," Jenny said with utter surety.

I felt a warmth on my chest where my necklace hung. I looked closely, and sure enough, I could see faint red and green light shining from under the necklines of their t-shirts.

"Yeah," I said, completing the handshake. "We've got this."

On Halloween night, the five of us headed out. We stopped at a few houses, as cover … and, I won't lie, for a little sugar high. Chocolate is good in times of stress, to this I can attest. David insisted on bringing his boom box, and he'd made a mixtape of dippy Halloween songs, Monster Mash, Purple People Eater, and the theme from the Addams Family TV show. Every time we passed some group of little kids, he'd dance around and make everybody laugh.

"I can't believe you're risking your boombox tonight!" I whispered to him at one point during our walk.

"What if it gets messed up?"

He laughed a strange laugh. "It's not mine! It's the one Mitch had in the garage!"

I started to frown and then decided that Mitch's belongings couldn't go to a better use than protecting people from an angry ghost. I returned his grin and resettled my candy bag on my arm. It was heavy, not with candy, but supplies for tonight's planned events.

By the time we got to the school, it was fully dark. We went in through one of the doors on the east side, near the gyms. Lorraine cast a fast spell first that she said would help us be less noticeable to anyone who might look out a window or drive by while we went through the keys on the principal's keyring to find the right one. Mr. Rakow had an impressive array of flashlights at his house and had provided us with one each for tonight, as well as a stand-up lantern for Jen's mom to use while she set up her spell. He used one of the smaller ones to work his way through trying each key in the lock.

I had privately wondered if I needed one of Mr. Rakow's lanterns for what I had in mind, but then thought better of it. I'd spent all of Friday night and Saturday practicing to make it all come together quickly, and I thought I could pull it off without any added light. Besides, I had enough stuff to carry as it was.

We found the right key pretty quickly, anyway. Mr. Rakow thought the larger ones were probably for exterior doors, and he was right. We slipped into the darkened hallway. I had been thinking it would be totally dark in here, but there was a tiny bit of reddish light cast by the EXIT signs at each end of the hallway we were in. It's remarkable the difference even a tiny bit of light can make in a dark situation.

We each had a job to do, and we'd been over it and over it so many thousands of times in the last two weeks, it was totally ingrained in my brain by now. Which turned out to be a very good thing, as once we got inside the building my adrenaline level shot up so high I was hard pressed to keep a coherent thought in my head at all.

The plan, though, rehearsed so many times, was my anchor. First move, walkie check. We each pulled out a walkie-talkie, provided by my dad, although he thought we were going to be using them to stay together while out trick-or-treating. So, yeah, technically not lying to my dad. *Gulp.* Everyone's check sounded loud in the silent hallway, making me even edgier, but they all worked, so we were good to go and trotted on down the hallway.

Lorraine peeled off first, after a quick blown kiss to all of us, and a hard hug for Jen. David stayed behind with her. His first job was to watch her back while she set up, and once she was good to go, he would move on to his phase two.

Jenny, Mr. Rakow and I trotted up the ramp that separated the gyms from the main part of the building. Jen and I went ahead, and Mr. Rakow paused here and there to begin laying out the first of the series of traps we'd planned for Charlie and his Ford.

It was a long jog down that hall in the dark, and I used it to remind myself to breathe normally. We got to a spot in front of the library that was about equidistant from the south and west doors. We weren't sure from which direction Charlie would make his entrance, so we'd calculated this spot as giving us the most warning, regardless.

Unless he just materializes full blown right in front of you and you get zero warning, the worried voice inside my head badgered me. *We have that contingency covered too, asshole,* I told the worried voice. *Chill out. We've got this.*

My worried voice wasn't wrong to be worried. David had been sharing the research he'd done on Charlie with me, and I'd taken to supplying him with stuff from the library. When she'd looked concerned about my sudden interest, I'd had to reassure Jeanne, my awesome librarian, that it was all legit research for a school history project.

She told me the story of what her folks were doing the week of Starkweather's rampage, how everyone in town had just been so scared and running around with guns, and when the whole story came out, how completely horrified and sad everyone was. I think she had experienced more people asking about him who were thinking of it as some glorious romantic 1950's tragic drama, than who were interested in the reality of it. She wanted, I think, for me to be sure that I was consuming the information with the proper amount of respect.

I thought about that a lot. I thought about how angry his ghost was, and the horrible, slithery feeling I'd had when I discovered the Kewpie doll in my backpack. I thought about Caril too, about how some people were just as mad at her as they were at Charlie, but how nobody knew for sure if she was a murderer too, or if she was just another of Charlie's victims. I thought maybe those people were just as bad as the ones who wanted to romanticize things, not because of how they felt about her, but because their continuing speculation about it just kept the pot stirred up.

I thought about all the people who got killed, Mr. Colvert who was in the Navy before he came home and got married. His wife was pregnant with a little girl when Charlie murdered him. That little girl never knew her dad because of Charlie. I thought about Caril's parents, Marion and Velda, and how when everything was all over with, Charlie had completely devastated that family. How could anybody even begin to put the pieces back together after something like that? Then there was the baby. Caril's little half-sister, Betty Jean. That was the worst.

There was just no way around it. If there was any way before he killed that little two-year-old girl, that Charlie wasn't a monster, then that sealed the deal right there. You don't kill a child that young in cold blood and stay the same person ever again. You just don't. He passed beyond forgivable-ness at that point for me. I'll make a lot of allowances for the vagaries of Charlie's childhood - poverty, bullies, the whole shebang of a shitty childhood that can explain why a lot of people are messed up. But that ended with Betty Jean.

August Meyer was a kind man. He stayed on his farm so his mother wouldn't have to move to a nursing home and could live out her life in her own, comfortable house. Bobby Jensen survived childhood polio, was bedridden most of his fifth-grade year and came out of it a kind and thoughtful boy who collected pencils, of all things. He was loved at home and also at school. He had an absolute sweetheart of a girlfriend in Carol King. The two of them had stopped to help Charlie and Caril when they had car trouble. Their good deed got them both killed.

Then there were the Wards. C. Lauer Ward was a kind man, a good boss, and good to his family. His wife, Clara was a pianist. She was a musician, like me. Their housekeeper, Lillian Fencl. She'd worked for the family for a long time and was well loved. Shy and quiet, she never would have caused Charlie any trouble. She was not a threat. He killed her anyway.

And his final victim, Merle Collison was killed in his sleep. In his sleep. Just so they could steal his car. The man was a soldier. A paratrooper in World War II. He fought and survived freaking Hitler's army, and came home to be killed in his sleep by a boy who was too dumb and too bored to be bothered to fight down the evil in his own soul. A boy whose entire legacy is one of horror and sadness and loss.

And now, here that boy was, trying to make a comeback. Wasn't it enough, the evil he'd already loosed on this town? Now he wanted to come back and start up again?

Not on our watch.

He wanted Caril, and he'd locked his sights on me. Well, okay, Charlie. Here's your chance to dance. I'm all dressed up and ready for you, you monster. I'm willing to bet that your badass 1950's self isn't going to know what to do with a badass 1980's girl.

I stopped in the center of the hallway. Jen and Mr. Rakow jogged down the hall to the left. I knelt and positioned my flashlight so I could see inside my bag. First thing I did was make my salt circle and close it up. I wasn't taking any chances that Charlie wouldn't make an appearance early and I didn't want him sneaking up on me without whatever protection the circle might give me intact.

With that done, I carefully laid out the items I'd brought with me. I already had my water guns filled with holy water strapped to my sides. Mr. Rakow had fashioned me a shoulder holster out of clothesline that worked surprisingly well, and it was easy enough to conceal under my cardigan. My mom never noticed it, even when we swung by the house at her request, so she could get a picture of the three of us in our costumes.

I'm sure they turned out great. David in some army pants and a t-shirt that miraculously fit Mr. Rakow way back in basic training, sporting the Rambo sweatband, at Jen's insistence. Even David couldn't say no to Jennifer. Jen in her khaki Alien spaceship-style jumpsuit, her dark hair pulled back so it looked short, and me in one of my mom's 50's skirts that already had a tear in it so she'd allowed me to have Aunt Mary alter it into something that still looked like a full skirt, but was, in fact, more like riding pants, so that I could run, unencumbered. With that, a little white top with a peter pan collar, and my hair up in a ponytail doing my very best to look like the object of Charlie's desire.

I set out the small, white candles Lorraine had provided for me, pre-blessed, and lit them. Then I waited. Until everyone was in place, all I had to do was wait. One by one, they checked in on the walkie-talkies. Mr. Rakow had hit all of the entrances with his booby traps and was in position in the doorway of the office. Jen checked in from her location in the main janitorial supply room. Jens' mom signaled that she was ready, her walkie signal significantly broken up, but still audible. We'd run into that issue when we'd tested using the walkies from inside the salt circles. The circle interfered with the reception some, and increasingly so as you added additional circles, but we determined that we would still be able to hear one another well enough to make them worth using. David was the last to check in, and I saw him coming back up from the gym area, breathing just a little heavily, but not much, considering the running I knew he'd just done.

He stopped in his pre-arranged location in front of the library doors and nodded. We had done everything in our power to combat the problems Jen had foreseen - the car, the destruction of the spell materials, and the fire. We were ready, and it was time. I was on.

The basic plan was this: I was the bait. I would use his attraction to me to draw him into the school. Once inside, we would first disable the car. We were operating under the assumption that the car was nearly as much of a threat to us on its own, as was Charlie. So, the first tactic was to take it out of the equation. After that, we would unleash the binding spell, immobilizing Charlie's ghost, then Lorraine would work her final mojo and get his butt banished.

I took a deep, cleansing breath in and out and started. I brought out the box of things I'd been pulling together over the last few weeks. I'd gotten a lot of it from thrift stores and the Army/Navy surplus store. I didn't know if my first solo attempt at spell-casting was going to have any impact at all, but with the help of the magic book from Melanie, I was game to try. I unwrapped the box, laying the white, square cloth napkin down first. I took the things out of the box one at a time and lay them out on the cloth. I worked quickly but deliberately, like I'd practiced, and whispered each name as I went.

"For Robert Colvert," I carefully laid down a badge from a Navy uniform, Petty officer, third class.

"For Marion Bartlett, Velda Bartlett and little Betty Jean," I carefully stacked three alphabet blocks in a triangle and put two very simple gold bands on the bottom two.

"For August Meyer," a handful of dried corn kernels.

"For Bobby Jensen," an old wooden pencil, "and for Carol King," a braid of strings from a cheerleader's pom-poms, in blue and red.

"For C. Lauer Ward and Clara Ward," a page of sheet music for the piano and a fancy looking cigar.

"For Lillian Fencl," I placed a white lily on the sheet music.

"And for Merle Collison," another uniform patch, this one jump wings.

I looked at the items there, laid out on the square of white cloth. I wiped a tear from my cheek and squared my shoulders.

"And finally, for Caril and for me." I drew out the Kewpie doll Charlie had deposited in my backpack. I stood then, turning around and around inside my little circle of protection. I took the head of the doll in one hand, its body in the other, and wrenched them apart. "Come on out, Charlie!" I shouted, "It's time to face the music!"

That was David's cue. Jen had carried in the boom box and set it at the library doors for David to use when he got inside. He had it all cued up already, and the volume cranked so when he hit play, the screaming guitar of Metallica's *Seek and Destroy* started pouring out.

I turned, scanning each of the doorways, the long hallways, trying to keep my eyes peeled in every direction, my heartbeat racing along with the music.

Nothing. Nothing nothing nothing. The moment stretched and stretched, I was on the verge of freaking out. All this work, all this planning, was he just going to blow us off? I screamed my frustration and anxiety along with the music. "Come on, Charlie you damned peckerwood!"

Then I heard it, the low throated rumble of that old Ford engine, but from where? Outside? Inside? The sound felt like it was coming from inside my head, vibrating in my jaw, threatening to stop my heart. Then, came the explosive crash of Detroit steel meeting public school fire door and the scream of twisting metal. I spun and finally located the sound. He was coming in from the north doors, down by the gym. I had a bare second to hope with all my heart that Lorraine was safely hidden tucked away in the girls' locker room before the Black 1949 Ford with the gaping hole where the grille should be, came blasting up the ramp between me and the gyms like it was powered by the fires of hell.

It ran over the first of three lines of spike strips Mr. Rakow had made from flat soaker hoses and nails right as it came inside the doors. It encountered the second row at the top of the ramp, and the third one as it came flying toward the office.

I desperately wanted to flee, to get the hell out of the way, but I didn't. Instead, I dropped the halves of the Kewpie doll to the ground and snatched my holy water guns out of their holster. I stood my ground.

The spike strips were effective; I could see from here the tires were damaged. But the car wasn't stopping. Had we relied entirely on those, I probably would have been done for right then. Fortunately, the name of this game was redundancy, and the backup plan was already in effect.

The Ford hit the slick of motor oil with which Mr. Rakow had coated the front hall. The Ford lost its grip on the hallway floor and went into a spectacular spin. I held my breath. Miraculously, before it got any closer to me, it slammed into the wall of the school office and came to a rest, front end crunched into the wall, both the hood and trunk springing open, the tires nearly flat.

The minute the car stopped, David jumped out of the shadows to my left and sprinted for the rear of the car, one hand clutching three hacky sacks. He tried to avoid the oil, but hit it, and slid into the car like a base runner. He caught himself with one hand on the Ford's bumper and with the other, crammed all three hacky sacks into the tailpipe. I'd been worried that they wouldn't stay put once they got inside, so Jen had come up with the idea of slitting them open and putting magnets inside.

At the same time, from his position in the shadows, Mr. Rakow shot out, holy water gun in one hand, a glob of something dark with wires sticking out in the other hand. This genius little thing was called a sticky bomb. It was basically a bunch of M-80 fireworks fused together and stuck into a chunk of sticky clay. You lit it, stuck it to whatever you wanted to blow, and got the hell out of the way.

Like all our tactics, we weren't sure what it would do to the car. We didn't know if it would do any damage at all, but even from here I could see that the holy water in the squirt gun was having an impact. Long, white, smoking wounds opened up on the body of the car everywhere Mr. Rakow had sprayed it.

My heart sang when I saw David getting away cleanly, tearing silently down the hallway toward the gyms, the way Charlie had entered.

In order to combat Jenny's prophecy that showed Charlie breaking our spell circle and ruining our plan, we'd devised a system of concentric circles to protect the spell – and the spellcaster. Lorraine was casting inside a double circle in the girl's locker room, which was inside the larger circle David had made outside, around the entire school. The idea was that whichever way Charlie entered the school, he would break the outer circle, but Lorraine's casting, inside her smaller circle, would stay intact. Once we had his entry point, David could repair the circle in that place, and reseal the entire school. Then Lorraine could break open her small circles and let the spell loose into the entire school.

We had gotten it to work beautifully on a smaller scale, but even the largest test we'd been able to do had covered maybe a quarter the distance we were working with tonight. For the millionth time that day, I crossed my fingers.

Then the car moaned. I stared at it in horror. I think what I was hearing was Charlie trying to start the car, but it didn't sound mechanical. It sounded animal. It heaved and moaned again. The sound made every hair on my body not just stand up, but try to flee.

I looked around for Mr. Rakow and saw him crouching, with a clear line of sight to the driver's side door. He had a loaded squirt gun in one hand, and his machete in the other. I'd seen the machete when he secured it in a leg sheath, but I hadn't looked at it too closely. From here, I caught a glimpse of the blade. There was light emanating from it, a reddish light, from a long, sinewy scar that ran the length of the blade. I couldn't be sure, but my impression was that it looked like a dragon.

The car howled. Inside the car, Charlie screamed. The hacky sacks must be working, or the holy water, or both, because the car wouldn't start. I wanted to cheer, and then Charlie burst from the car, and all cheer vanished.

In life, Charlie was a little guy. He was short, bowlegged and red-headed, doing his best James Dean. In death, even those elements of humanity had escaped him. The thing that emerged from the car wasn't man-shaped at all. It was dark and jagged; an irregular mass bound together with barbed bands of glowing electricity. And it screamed.

When Charlie jumped from the car, Mr. Rakow had taken a defensive posture between him and me, anticipating an immediate attack. Instead, strangely, Charlie focused his ire on the car.

Saying *that* was a bizarre sight would definitely be grading on a curve, at this point, but for a tiny second, I almost laughed. Charlie flipped out on his car! He screamed at it, flailed at it, struck it, like a dude on steroids whose ride has just wronged him. He wailed and stomped what passed for feet. Then to complete the ridiculous scene, he kicked the tires.

I shot Mr. Rakow a wide-eyed look. Mr. R wasn't

allowing himself to be distracted in the least, which turned out to be a blessing, because when Charlie did turn his attack toward us, Mr. Rakow was ready. I tried my best not to recoil and break my circle, to stay in position and be brave, like Mr. Rakow had. I forced myself to stay put and watch, and it was horrible.

Charlie attacked like a storm cloud. I honestly didn't understand how Mr. Rakow could either defend against it or attack. There didn't seem to be anything to target, no head, no heart. Flashes of jagged blackness shot out of it, striking at Mr. Rakow with blinding speed. He parried with the machete, a task it was not built for, but he managed. In fact, he was holding his own brilliantly.

I confess, until then I'd thought of Mr. Rakow as kind of old. I knew he was smart and clever and had seen a lot of action in the Army, but I thought of that as being further in the past. In that darkened junior high school hallway, I realized how wrong I was.

Mr. Rakow fought brilliantly. I'm not sure what fighting styles he'd studied, but there was something elegantly balletic about his movements. He parried the strikes coming from the dark mass that was Charlie like they were in slow motion. He spun, he ducked, he avoided more blows than I could count, and every time Charlie struck, Mr. Rakow struck back, either with shots from the holy water gun or his machete, now glowing bright red in the low light. The two danced across the hallway with darkly fascinating steps.

Then Charlie caught Mr. Rakow's sword arm, entangled it in his barbed blackness and drew him forward. I glimpsed Mr. Rakow's face and felt his pain. He didn't scream. He didn't need to. I did it for him.

Then, the sticky bomb underneath the Ford exploded. Truthfully, I'd forgotten about it entirely. I don't know how long that fuse burned, it seemed like forever, but it couldn't have been more than a minute or two. It wasn't a regular explosion, like any of this was regular.

The initial blast wave blew Mr. Rakow away from

Charlie and sent him crashing into the wall somewhere behind me. My ears sang with a high-pitched whine and I dropped to the ground. Remarkably, my circle held. Chunks of sticky flaming black goo struck clear space all around me and slid to the floor as if I was inside an invisible tube.

The wall separating the hall from the office didn't fare so well. It had already taken a severe hit when the Ford crashed into it, but now, flaming chunks of demon car were plastered to the wall and the whole thing was engulfed.

Several things happened in quick succession then. First, I felt the enormous surge of contained power when the circle around the outside of the school snapped up. David had done it! I grabbed my walkie-talkie and yelled into it, still unable to hear my own words over the high-pitched whine in my ears, hoping Jen's mom would get the message. "It's up! The circle is up!"

The second thing that happened was that I caught motion out of the corner of my eye. It was Jen. Her job had been to gather up all the fire extinguishers she could manage and bring them up to the main hallway. We'd played around with methods of transportation because more than two or three of those at once got pretty heavy to carry. We ended up with a fitted sheet she could drag behind her. It kept them from falling out and it was easy to pull. While everything else was hitting the fan, she had calmly managed to find nearly a dozen of them and bring them to the bottom of the stairway near the main hall.

She'd been crouching down there, just waiting for the fire she had foreseen. When the car blew, she acted. Her costume did a decent job of keeping her out of sight as she snaked along the wall toward the office, but not good enough. I spotted a sharp movement from the dark mass that was Charlie and knew I needed to do something to keep him distracted long enough for Jen to get to the fire, and for Lorraine to cut loose the binding spell.

Come on, Mom, I thought desperately to myself, *we're*

running out of tricks here, and I smudged my salt circle and stepped out. I hadn't realized how much of the chaos my circle was keeping out until the haze of acrid smoke and heat smacked me in the face.

"Hey, Charlie!" I shouted above the roar of the car fire. "C'mon, man! This is why you're here, isn't it? It's me you're here for!"

The blackness that was Charlie focused on me. My heart jackhammered in my chest. I held my squirt guns, one in each hand, and stood firm. Charlie gathered himself and charged.

Man, this was gonna hurt.

I had trained. I had planned. I knew there was going to be pain. I just didn't know how much. He didn't hit me so much as engulf me and we tumbled down the hallway, entwined. The heat was impossible. I didn't know anything could hurt that much. Every nerve-ending I had was shrieking in agony. I couldn't see, couldn't breathe. I did the only thing I could do, I pulled both triggers. Holy water jetted from my little guns directly into the dark mass and it screamed.

Then, suddenly, the pain was gone. I rolled until my momentum was spent and forced my eyes open. Mr. Rakow had positioned himself behind me so that when I rolled, he was there to meet Charlie. Through the red haze of my vision, I saw him, standing over Charlie, the machete grasped in both hands. He'd driven it through like a spike and impaled Charlie to the floor. The machete glowed darkly red.

The air changed. It became charged with a stillness, a sticky fullness. Lorraine's binding spell! It wrapped around the smoky dark blob pinned to the linoleum floor by Mr. Rakow's knife and pulled it up and away, where it hung, spinning about ten feet from the ground.

Mr. Rakow fell, and for the first time, I got a look at how injured he was. There was blood everywhere. I tried to crawl to him and couldn't force my limbs to move. I spotted Jen over by the office, tossing one fire extinguisher aside and grabbing the next one. Then my eye was drawn up again.

The binding spell still had Charlie immobilized, but he was fighting it. Bolts of lightning flashed from the darkness, the whole mass twisted and spun. Then the screaming began. The horrible noise jolted my body into motion. Ignoring the pain for the moment, I scuttled over to Mr. Rakow and was beyond relieved to discover that beneath the bleeding rents, he was alive.

"Are you ok, Mr. Rakow?" I croaked.

He nodded sharply and hissed at me, "He's fighting the binding spell!"

I looked up at the dark smudge that was Charlie. It was screaming and twisting, fighting to get free.

"Will it hold until she can banish him?"

A bolt of electricity shot out of the struggling mass and shattered the door leading into the library.

Crap crap crap "What do we do?" I implored. "Can you move?"

He tried and slipped back down in a slick of his own blood. I blanched.

"Jenny!" I yelled. She poked her head out of the smoking office and scoped out the situation. I reached a hand out to her and felt a *clunk* inside me, like some large piece of machinery had dropped into place. I had no clue what that meant, but it felt very strong and very right.

Then I noticed the light between us. It was glowing purple. I glanced down and saw my necklace shining like a floodlight. It was shooting a beam directly toward Jen's necklace, and where the two met in the middle, my blue light and her red one merged.

"Angie! Look!" rasped Mr. Rakow, pointing up. I looked, Charlie was cringing away from the beam of light.

My eyes locked on Jen's. She realized it the same second I did and grabbed her walkie-talkie off her belt and shouted into it, "David! We need you here! Now!"

He must have already been on his way toward us because he skidded into view almost before she ended the transmission. "Stop there!" I shouted, pointing at a spot opposite Charlie. The second I pointed at him, a second shaft of blue light erupted from my necklace toward him. It was caught midway by a beam of green light from his necklace, merging into a deep ocean shade. On his other side, I caught a glimpse of the beams connecting Jenny and David. They didn't blend as much as swirl. There was a metallic sheen to it. Once all three corners were in place, the triangle of light broadened and grew brighter.

Charlie screamed again, and a lightning bolt shot from the center of his darkness, but it couldn't escape the triangle. We were holding him! The power of the Triad! Just like the ghosty lady said! I was so psyched - I could feel power running through us like a circuit, and it felt awesome! We had this! We could hold him!

I felt a second wave of power roll through the school, coming up from the gym where Jens' mom was doing her spellcasting. It had to be the banishing spell! It was going to work! It had to! I watched as the banishing spell took hold of Charlie and the darkness began to fade to gray. Tendrils began lifting out and away from the center of his mass as if they were being pulled.

We watched, fascinated as the shape began to pull apart, long snaky fingers of smoke trying to hold the center and being sucked downward.

Hope flashed through me. It all looked like it was all going so well, until from one heartbeat to the next, I couldn't breathe. One tiny, thin tendril of that darkness had snaked out and seized me around the neck. It yanked me forward, hard. I tumbled and caught myself on my hands and knees. I wanted to scream, needed to breathe, and couldn't. I felt a hand on my ankle, Mr. Rakow, battered and bleeding behind me was trying to drag me back.

My vision started to darken and I saw David shoot forward like he was coming for me. The triangle of light wavered and I waved my hands desperately at him to stop. We couldn't let go, we had to keep him inside the triangle! My left hand flailed at my neck, trying to push

Charlie away, but there was only smoke - nothing I could grasp. My blue light was fading. The world was receding to a pinprick, and then, I began to hear voices.

She's trying to help! It sounded like a girl's voice, maybe a little older than me.

She's not strong enough, nobody is strong enough! That voice was different, older, wearier.

They need us! The voices got muddled, like a group of people talking in the next room.

How can we help?

Help the girl breathe!

Then a tiny voice, like a child's but so insistent, *Need granny!* The tiny voice cried out, *Granny!!*

Then darkness for a second that stretched out, so long, so painfully long. I was on the ground, on my hands and knees, head down, necklace brushing the linoleum floor tiles and...

AIR!

Sweet air filled my lungs in a rush! The acrid, smoke-smelling nasty air was gone. This was sweet, flower garden after a spring rainstorm sweet, sweet air.

I lifted my head and looked up at the angry darkness that was Charlie. I thought for a moment, I could see eyes boring into me, but it might have been spots in my vision. That sweet air, though, that was no illusion. I barked out a triumphant shout and an explosion of purple smoke engulfed the air within the triangle and *shoved* at Charlie. It shoved him down in the direction the spell was trying to take him, down, away from us.

Charlie screamed again and I heard a familiar voice, my brain scrambled for focus, oxygen still flooding back in, who was that voice?

Git! The voice flooded my ears, my head, my heart. *You will harm no more innocents this day!* The voice was old and strong. So strong. All the other voices seemed to cling to her, lending their strength. Her voice grew even stronger. *Be Gone! Back to the Hell from whence you came! Be GONE!*

And whoosh! Just like those commercials that show your yucky hair clog vanishing down the drain, all the darkness that was Charlie whooshed down and away, right down through the floor of the main hallway of our school. I almost breathed a sigh of relief when I had to scuttle back out of the way as the Ford got dragged down after Charlie, metal bending and folding like the legs of an angry black beetle.

Then I collapsed. Jenny and David were at my side in a second, looking concerned, but mostly unhurt. I tried to raise my head and couldn't. Jen slid her legs under me and cradled my head in her lap.

She reached inside her coverall and pulled out a first aid kit. She handed it to David who slid over to see to Mr. Rakow. I was gazing dumbly at the purple smoke receding upwards. My head was still foggy, the voices were fading to a murmur, all but one. It was the ghosty lady from the day we'd helped David save Frankie from Charlie and his Ford. She stood a little bit away from us, surrounded by an aura of fragrant purple, her coat and hat unrumpled. She pinned me with a stare.

Good work, child.

"Thank you," my voice came out in a hoarse whisper. "Thank you for helping us; for helping them." Jen cocked her head at me and followed my eyes until she too, spotted the old woman. I felt her turn and motion to David and Mr. Rakow.

The storm loosed him, but you lot have put him back in his box. We can take it from here. She smiled at me and pointed. *You wear that well, child.*

And she was gone. I looked at where she pointed and remembered I'd pinned the purple pansy from Melanie's magical apothecary cabinet to my cardigan.

Pansy...

Lorraine came sprinting up about then, and before too many more minutes passed, there were firefighters and EMTs rushing around. Mr. Rakow got carried out on a stretcher. Charlie had sliced him up pretty good. He was bleeding from a dozen wounds, but she said they told her he would be ok once they got him all stitched up.

By then I was outside, sitting in the back of an open ambulance. My neck was blossoming with bruises, and a police officer was standing by to take my statement. I marveled as Jen explained with a totally straight face how I'd gotten the bruises cutting through somebody's side yard and getting hung up on their clothesline. The rest of the explanation was trickier though. Coming upon the school, hearing a disturbance inside and Mr. Rakow being attacked by the vandals was about the best we could come up with.

I think there would have been a lot more questions asked, if it hadn't been for Officer Yardley. He'd been our neighborhood cop forever and was one of the officers who responded this summer when we had our run-in with demon-possessed Mitch. I got the distinct feeling that he knew more than he was letting on and was ok with us glossing things over for the time being. I suspected we hadn't heard the last from him, though.

It was David who finally put the pieces together afterward. The ghosty woman who helped us, all the clues about grandmothers and pansies, it all pointed to Pansy Brooks, Caril's grandmother. She was the one who never trusted Charlie to begin with. She was the one who sent the police over to her daughter and son-in-law's house when they hadn't been seen in a week. Once we made the connection, Jen realized that it was Pansy's gravestone where she'd ended up at the end of her first prophecy back at Wyuka. We'd all been so focused on Charlie, and Caril's grandmother had been such a small part of his story, that we hadn't clicked on it until the end.

I didn't tell Jen and David right away about the other voices I'd heard. That was the part of my plan the magic book from Melanie had helped me with. I hadn't told them everything about the book either, because I wasn't quite sure I wanted to share it yet. I would, in time, but it was so personal at first, I wanted to keep it close.

Following the book's instructions, I had attempted to magically call forth the spirits of Charlie's victims. I wasn't sure it would work, even with the help of Phyllida's spells. I was no real practitioner of magic. I was just a kid with a book.

I'd needed to gamble on it, though. Charlie's spirit was so strong, I truly believed that it was going to take more than the sum of all our parts to banish him. Phyllida's book helped me to understand that because of how magic worked, the people most able to help us make it happen would be the people he'd wronged. I really wanted it to work, too. Not just for us, in the present, but for them. I know for a fact if it was me in their shoes, I'd have wanted the chance to put Charlie down for good. And when I say Phyllida's book helped me, I mean that in a very active sense. The first time I'd opened the book, it had spoken to me. Not aloud, but writing appeared on pages that at first had seemed blank, and later, comments would emerge in the margins of a page I was looking at. The ink was always the same - a bright, shiny purple.

That day I opened the book for the very first time, this is what greeted me, the words surfacing from the page as if they were rising to the top of a pool:

Dear Angie,

You hold in your hands a great tome of massive power. You must not use this for ill will or you will be damned to the darkest pits of the most evil places...

I'm kidding. You've found this book or it has landed in your hands for a reason. First of all, don't panic. Right now, you're asking yourself, "How does this book know that I panic a

I learned quite a few things from the book, not the
least of which was, the book was kind of a smartass. But,
it helped me figure out which spells to use to call to Charlie's victims, and how to create a space for them to help if
they could. It's helped me innumerable times since, as
well, so I tolerate its smartassedness with good humor.

The one final thing that kept waking me up at night,
searching through the book and every other source I
could get my hands on, was the nature of the storm that
had awakened Charlie in the first place. We'd never determined if that was something fluky, or if it had been a deliberate act, and if it had been deliberate, who, or what,
was behind it? What monstrous evil had that sort of
power?
     It was a question I wouldn't be able to answer for
some time, and rest assured, it wasn't an answer any of us
were going to like.

BIBLIOGRAPHY

Dyer, E. (1993). Headline: Starkweather: From behind the news desk. Lincoln, NE: Journal-Star Print. Co.
Kelly, B., Stearns, D. O., Hamer, D., Hinchik, S., Falk, B., Beaver, N., & WOWT (Television station : Omaha, Neb.). (1990). Charles and Caril: Starkweather 30 years later.

Kurtis, B., Columbia House Video Library., Columbia TriStar Home Video (Firm), & Arts and Entertainment Network. (1994). *American justice: Bonnie & Clyde, Charles Starkweather*. Terre Haute, IN: Columbia House Video Library [distributor.

Malick, T., Sheen, M., Spacek, S., Oates, W., Probyn, B., Fujimoto, T., Larner, S., ... Warner Home Video (Firm). (1999). Badlands. Burbank, CA: Warner Home Video.

McArthur, J. (2012). Pro Bono: The 18-year defense of Caril Ann Fugate.

O'Donnell, J. (1993). Starkweather: A story of mass murder on the Great Plains. Lincoln, NE: J & L Lee Publishers.

Roth, T., Balk, F., Quaid, R., Dennehy, B., Hickox, S. B., Markowitz, R., New World International (Firm), ... Malofilm Video (Firm). (1993). *Murder in the heartland.* Canada: Malofilm Video.

ALSO

Special Collection of clippings and ephemera located in
the Heritage Room of Nebraska Authors: http://lin-
colnlibraries.org/reference-services/starkweather/

Jones, D. R. (2008-2018). Personal interviews.

About the Author

Sarah Dale is an author, mom, partner, daughter, step-mom, friend, dog-walker, cat-appreciator, library book-balancer, word lover, think-thinker and picture-taker living in Lincoln, Nebraska, and just generally trying to get things done.

www.sarahdaleauthor.com

Facebook: facebook.com/wecouldbeheroesnovel/

Twitter: @sarahdaleauthor

Instagram: instagram.com/wecouldbeheroesnovel/

Goodreads: goodreads.com/stillphoenix

Amazon: amazon.com/author/stillphoenix

Other titles you might enjoy from Snowy Wings Publishing

A Haunting in Hollowfield
-Jennie K. Brown

https://www.snowywingspublishing.com/book/a-haunt-ing-in-hollowfield/

A Touch of Magic
-Janina Franck

https://www.snowywingspublishing.com/book/a-touch-of-magic/

Different Worlds
-Lyssa Chiavari

https://www.snowywingspublishing.com/book/differ-ent-worlds/

www.ingramcontent.com/pod-product-compliance
Lightning Source LLC
Chambersburg PA
CBHW032046180726
48284CB00004B/1210